Arrival

by

H J Perry

AF613198

Arrival © H J Perry 2015
this edition edited & published 2022
All rights reserved. No part of this story may be used, reproduced or transmitted in any form or by any means without written permission of the copyright holder, except in the case of brief quotations embodied within critical reviews and articles.
This book is a work of fiction. The names, characters, places, and incidents are products of the writer's imagination or have been used fictitiously and are not to be construed as real. Any resemblance to persons, living or dead, actual events, locale or organizations is entirely coincidental.
The author has asserted his/her rights under the Copyright Designs and Patents Acts 1988 (as amended) to be identified as the author of this book.
Written in American English.
www.HelenJPerry.com

ABOUT *Arrival: a gay romance in a Post Apocalyptic Dystopian Society*

Forbidden love.

What if men and women lived in separate asexual communities?

It is seven decades after the pandemic and the population is still teetering on the brink of extinction. Most people are infertile, and male babies are rare. Adult males are generally impotent and lethargic, a consequence of altered DNA.

A minority of people still crave physical, sexual pleasure. The West Beach fertility unit doubles as a brothel for deviants, women who desire men.

Alton and Paul are among the minority of men who are virile.

The Matriarchal society doesn't work in the interests of all citizens.

When Alton leaves his rural male community, he is shocked to discover he is expected to provide sexual services to wealthy women. He can't do it. He has someone special on his mind. Alton feels more than brotherly love for his lifelong friend. After five months apart they will be reunited but does Paul feel the same?

Contains hot young men getting sexy together. All characters in the book are over 18.

Speculative fiction meets M/M romance in a post-apocalyptic dystopian Matriarchy.

*** 2016 Rainbow Awards: Honorable Mention ***

Read Arrival by HJ Perry now

CHAPTER ONE
Foresters

As a nineteen-year-old, if only by one week, Alton was eligible. With hours to wait until the announcement, he tossed and turned in bed.

A community elder would deliver the declaration after breakfast to the gathered teenagers, as was customary. After which, word would quickly spread through the populace.

For months, since Paul left for West Beach near the Capital, Alton clung to optimistic anticipation, hoping he would be one of the chosen few who would follow.

Every time, the same routine. Twice, sometimes three times a year, a ship bringing supplies from The Capital docked without warning in the decrepit old harbor. The sleepy colony transformed into a hive of activity as men and boys answered the call to unload the cargo, greet the guests, and meet the new guards.

Weather permitting, within just a few turns of the tide, the ship would set sail again, returning south, taking away the guards who had served their time and any young men selected for transfer.

A mixture of excitement and apprehension always preceded the much-anticipated event. Some teenagers craved the excitement, the adventure of leaving their rural life behind to travel and live near the faraway city, and the promise of a better life.

Status went with being a Foresters' hero. The absent men who sent the shipments of paper, pencils, clothes, and other luxuries were heroes and always celebrated at formal community gatherings. All elements that featured in the farewell speech, every time. Not everyone wanted to go, of course; most didn't because life within the men's community was all they'd ever known.

Only eight youths at The Foresters were eligible this time by virtue of their age, and maybe none of them would be chosen.

Despite the fear of the unknown, Alton wanted—no, needed—to be chosen more than anything. This wasn't his only opportunity; there would be a couple more ships before his twentieth birthday and Paul was half a year older at the time when he left. Alton didn't want to delay; he longed to follow in Paul's footsteps. No man left after reaching twenty years of age.

Lying there was pointless. Unanswerable questions mingled with doubt in his mind. He cast a glance at the empty bed across the room, as he had every morning for the past five months. The same bed that Alton had shared year after year on the coldest winter nights with Paul.

From infancy, the only way to survive the harsh cold winters, especially the long dark nights, was to share body heat. Young boys slept two or three in a bed on the bitterest of nights. They weren't big beds, so in recent years Paul and Alton struggled to sleep together as they grew into men. One of them fell out in the night, crashing onto the floor on more than one occasion.

Regardless of the fuel burnt, the open hearths were not powerful enough to counteract the biting icy fingers of the cold air. It whipped throughout the farmhouse, which was now the sleeping quarters of twenty-four men and boys.

All the buildings on the farm and throughout the small town predated the pandemic Matriarchy, making even the most modern more than seventy years old.

After the pandemic had taken humanity to the brink of extinction, there were plenty of empty structures to utilize and little point or manpower to begin new construction projects. The community used what houses were available but with minimal maintenance, even the most efficient were suffering deterioration.

The brief hours of darkness gave way to warm summer sunlight penetrating the threadbare window dressings. The noisy dawn chorus subsided and anyone awake must wonder how others slept through the morning commotion made by the birds.

Moving slowly and silently, Alton got out of bed and pulled on his clothes. He took care not to wake the other boys in his room before leaving to find some useful occupation for the early morning.

At all times of day and night on a large farm, something needed doing and Alton needed to do something to pass the time.

Two new baby boys had arrived on the ship, babies can awaken at any hour. Alton paused outside the nursery and listened for any sound to interrupt the silence. Everyone was sleeping in the old house. The boys' quarters were at the center of the territory, where all could keep a watchful eye over them.

Alton crept along the landing, tiptoed down the stairs, and walked to the front door. He pulled it open and stepped into the crisp morning air, taking care to close the door quietly behind him.

A morning mist rolled across the vista, swirling inland from the sea, but the summer sun would soon burn it off leaving just a lining of wet morning dew for those who rose later from their slumber. Just a hint of sea salt flavored the air.

The kitchen and mess hall, located in a former barn, were a short walk across the courtyard. As the hub of the community, the place where they came together to eat had undergone considerable alteration and modernization, making it the only well-insulated all-weather structure. Breakfast preparations would be underway, even at this early hour. It was an enormous task to feed the town of more than two thousand people at every meal.

"You're up early, Alton." A female voice cut through the sounds of early morning nature.

He looked across the courtyard to see the guard approaching, her white uniform dazzlingly bright in the morning sunlight.

"So are you." Alton stopped walking, waiting for Barb to draw near. "Are you leaving today?"

"I am. I'm going home to The Capital," Barb replied in a hushed voice but with unmistakable excitement. "But first I've got to train my replacement. She needs to be able to administer the meds each morning without waiting for the doctor."

"The doctor's not leaving yet, is she?" He started to move again, walking alongside her toward the mess hall.

"No. She's staying for the winter but will have a new guard to work with."

The female guards kept themselves to themselves, with little interaction between them and the permanent residents, the men, and boys. Except at the daily medication handout. Medical matters, one of only two tasks entrusted to outsiders, to women. That and guarding the town against invaders. Not that the isolated town needed guarding.

In Alton's entire lifetime, The Foresters had received no hostile visitors. They had no neighbors and no roads into the locality. No human habitat for hundreds of miles beyond the farmland and the dense forest that had grown up, concealing the remaining traces of the past civilization.

"This morning's meds will probably be the last time I see you then," said Alton.

"Aren't you coming with us today? You're nineteen now, aren't you?" Barb asked.

"Yes, I'm nineteen. My birthday was last week. But we don't know who's going; the announcement is later today," Alton replied.

"Ah, yes. I remember. So you have no idea which boys will be traveling with us. We're supposed to set sail this afternoon with the tide. I hope I will see you on board."

They arrived at the door of the mess hall together, and Alton slowed to a halt. He wanted to ask so many questions, stuff a guard might be able to answer.

"Shall we go in?" She placed her hand on the door handle, unaware of his concerns.

"If I am on board, what sort of place will I be going to?" he blurted out before they were forced to split up once inside.

"I don't know. Honestly, I don't. I've never been to West Beach, and I don't know anyone who has. But it will be a good place for you." Barb pulled open the door and walked in, going directly to the table in the near corner, where traditionally females sat and ate.

Alton continued past, heading toward the kitchen and the yeasty aroma of freshly baked bread. Rows of loaves and buns sat cooling on racks, but the two bakers were both kneading, almost up to their elbows in flour and sticky dough. They worked in silence. What could they have to say to each other when they did this same thing day after day while most slept?

Alton could never imagine himself working in the kitchen on such a repetitive task.

Without a word, he walked through to the cold storeroom, constructed on the northern face of the building, to fetch supplies for the day, sacks of potatoes and carrots, drums of milk, baskets of eggs. Later in the day, a team would harvest lettuce and cucumber later and bring them to the kitchen for preparation, ready to eat fresh from the ground.

Alton had made several journeys carting stock to and fro from the store when the head baker finally spoke.

"I'll be seeing you at the announcement," said Peter, while liberating fresh loaves from their tins.

"Why?" Alton turned to face the bakers, with a basket of eggs still in their hands.

"Because I'm the one doing the announcing," Peter said, as if this was no big deal.

"Do you know if I'm down?"

"I'm sure I couldn't say if I did know, but no, I don't." He set the final loaf down on the rack and started clinking and clattering the empty bread tins as he gathered them.

"I don't think you should announce his name if you've got any say in the matter," the other baker, Ted, chipped in. Ted was older, much older, than Peter.

"Why?" Alton and Peter both asked.

Alton still remembered sharing a room with Peter back in the day when Peter seemed tall and grown-up. Ten years ago Peter left the youngsters' home to sleep in one of the adult dwellings. A tired Foresters' community elder might be Alton's fate in ten years' time.

"Because the kitchen'd miss him doing the heavy stuff in the mornings and I hear he's the muscle on the farm all day."

"Haven't you ever noticed, they usually choose the most useful men, the best swimmers, the fastest runners, the strongest javelin throwers? Our very best hunters?" Alton assumed others noticed this pattern, this common quality among the men who left.

"No." The bakers spoke in unison this time, both looking at Alton as if he had two heads.

Alton was equally incredulous. How did they not see?

A couple of days of excitement around the arrival of the boat interrupted months of lethargy. In the community, they lived a hand-to-mouth existence. Subsistence farming, with most men doing the bare minimum each day. The children were energetic, but as they turned into adults, they seemed drained of life and motivation.

In the past couple of years, Alton started to notice the selected youths often excelled in some way. The brightest and the best. The swiftest runners, archers with the most accurate aim. The tallest and the best sportsmen. Alton was none of these, so the likelihood of him following Paul, being transferred, didn't bode well, but he was healthy and hard working.

Since Paul left these past five months, Alton seized every opportunity to undertake all the physically hard labor. He wanted to fill his time and collapse into bed each night exhausted. Most of the time this worked.

Everyone knew Paul and Alton were the closest of friends, despite their differences.

They'd grown up together, and like brothers, they had contrasting temperaments and interests. As opposites, they seemed to work well together. Sporty, sociable, and outgoing, Paul contrasted with the quiet introvert of the partnership. Alton was happiest when engaged in solo activities and never drew attention to himself. He didn't waste words and wasn't interested in small talk. The younger boys followed and copied Paul, whereas Alton just existed as a face in the crowd but never the center of attention.

He remembered the last ship when Paul left.

"We're proud of him," people said of Paul.

They were always proud of the men that went away. Whatever they did, wherever they went, they were well rewarded. Those men paid for the goods that came to The Foresters on the ships. They paid for the guards and the doctor that worked in the community.

'This will be good for you. You can stop living in his shadow,' people said. Well-meaning men of the community and female guards made insensitive comments like this to Alton on the day of the last announcement. The day they discovered Paul had been selected to leave the community and never return.

Just because Paul shone brightly, Alton didn't feel he lived in the shade, he didn't crave the limelight.

'You'll be lost without Paul.'

No, not lost. Alton just didn't want to grow old in a town where over the period of ten years he would go from being a carefree kid to a young adult, but in the same timescale again he could turn into an elder. The baker had been a kid alongside Paul and Alton. He'd grown up in the same house with them but was an elder already.

Alton wanted to follow Paul.

Needed to follow him.

The people with the glib comments didn't understand. There were things he wanted to share with his best friend. Things he needed to say. Things that had been left unspoken.

In the days and weeks following Paul's departure, Alton realized he had to see Paul again, to tell him.

CHAPTER TWO
Alton

While they were most apprehensive about their mysterious destination, the journey itself also gave cause for concern. They had heard tales of hostile encampments in areas that should have been unoccupied between the far-flung male habitats. Alton had no idea whether these were simply stories or based on truth.

Away from the safety in numbers offered by their remote home, they were an easy target for pirates or terrorists. Anarchist groups eeking out a subsistence living or female extremists who would prefer to end the men's units altogether.

The two men hoped for calm waters and no confrontation through the week-long voyage, sailing along the coastline.

The boys felt restless and impatient. Cooped up on a cramped boat with limited means of amusement soon became tedious. The youths were used to an active outdoor life, with the town and woods to roam in freely after completing daily work on the farm.

On the potentially perilous voyage, the men were not allowed on deck at any time lest they be seen from land or another boat. The crew and guards stayed constantly vigilant in ensuring the males remained hidden. There was no way they would be allowed to walk on solid ground, and the vessel maintained a good distance from the land for the whole voyage.

They soon found their sea legs, becoming accustomed to the constant motion of the boat rocking, rolling, bobbing over the rise and fall of the swell. Alton slept or pretended to sleep for ridiculously long hours, allowing his mind to enjoy daydreams as he tried to shut out the reality. He was somewhere between bored and crazy due to the inactivity, monotony, and constant flow of words from the other boy.

Alton would never have chosen Mark as a traveling companion. At home, he had found him loud and annoying. The sort of teenager who wanted to be the center of attention and youth leader but did nothing worthy of either, in Alton's opinion. To his amazement, many of the younger boys looked up to Mark.

It was incredible how simply having a big mouth and lack of self-awareness earned respect among gullible followers. The incessant chatter, full of hopes but no substance, became an annoying background hum, requiring little acknowledgment. Alton did not want to engage in pointless speculation; they had no idea what to expect at the end of this trip.

On a fine September morning, Alton and Mark were exhausted from the journey when they finally arrived at West Beach Men's Unit. They carried only small bags of personal treasures and the clothes they wore; faded threadbare garments that had been worn by numerous teenagers before them.

The guards from the boat, who had traveled with them from The Foresters, accompanied them to the reception area where they were all met by a resident guard of West Beach. A different men's unit, but the guards wore the same white and cream uniform. The guards dispersed, leaving the boys waiting and watching the four doors in the room.

The bright room was bare, with whitewashed walls and just a few wooden benches. Light entered through windows along two walls, but the windows were up by the high ceiling. Even if one man stood on the shoulders of the other, Alton doubted he'd be able to see out.

After a few very dull, uneventful minutes spent slumped on benches, Alton and Mark stood up when two more new arrivals joined them.

"Hello, I'm Cecil and this is Mo. We're from Eb's Farm," said one of the men, pointing to himself and then turning to his companion. They appeared tired and disheveled.

"Mark and Alton. Good to meet you." Mark spoke on behalf of them both and continued, "Do you know anything about this place?"

"Nah. I can only tell you Mo and I were the fittest and the tallest at Eb's, so that's us." Cecil raked his dark fingers through his scruffy black hair.

They all remained standing, shifting from one foot to another, Mo paced the room. After the long journey, finding feet on solid ground had never felt so good.

"You could just say we were the best, so it is no surprise we're picked." Mo's first words came out as cocky and confident, just like his companion. Both of them stood at over six feet, they were taller than Mark, and all three towered over Alton.

"Well, that explains me then. I'm one of the better specimens of Foresters, but I can't explain why short-arsed Alton's here," replied Mark. Alton forced himself to join them all in laughter at the joke.

"I've been told it's no coincidence that they're selective, as this is a center for human breeding and research into fertility. Of course, they will want the very best male specimens for that." Mo strutted like a peacock as if to demonstrate his bestness.

"Really? We weren't told anything," said Alton.

"Well, like I said, that would explain why I'm here." Mark appeared to enjoy the macho bonding that looked like it might easily escalate into a testosterone-fueled fight over superiority. The sort of conversation Alton would usually step back from, but here he was trapped in a new environment and determined to stand his ground in front of the two strangers.

"But that certainly can't be said of you, Alton. I can't guess why they picked you," Mark taunted, and the other boys laughed.

"Perhaps he's here for his good looks, like mine," Cecil jumped in to defuse the tension with a big smile and a wink.

"Perhaps they are looking for brains, but that's an area Mark's a bit short in." Alton delivered a harsh dig at Mark. Determined, the annoying companion would not get away with making him look foolish in front of everyone, especially as they had only just met these other boys.

"You can't call anyone short!" A quick-witted response from Mark.

"Now, now." Cecil held up his hands, palms outwards, carving out his role as a peacemaker.

"Well, you are a quiet, deep thinker." Mark turned to address the others, "If that's what they are looking for, Alton's the man for the job."

"Have others come from Foresters before you? The men we remember from Eb's were always the cream of the athletes," said Mo.

Paul, thought Alton, but he could not say the name; he could not say anything about the man he missed so much.

Words always poured out of Mark's mouth. Without taking up any thinking time, he replied, "Paul was the last guy from home to come here. He was my good buddy and, yeah, the same as us, tall, popular, great sports player. Just like me." He grinned and his brain must have caught up as he registered what he said.

Mark glanced at his travel companion. "And he was good friends with Alton too." Mark stared at Alton as if reading his thoughts, but his mouth kept going, "Paul was the life of the party; all the younger kids looked up to him."

Alton glared at Mark while irrational jealousy flared inside his overwrought mind.

"There are some good guys here from Eb's too, but there'll be men from all over. They don't have children growing up here, you know," said Cecil, still working hard to keep on friendly terms.

Oblivious to the conversation moving on, having found new potential allies, Mark continued to glare at Alton. "I never understood why Paul hung out with you, Alton. I don't mean to be rude, but..."

A sure sign of intentional rudeness is coming up.

"You gotta admit you're not like us. Not like Paul and me."

You and Paul do not go together, not in the same breath, not in the same sentence. You must be mad to think you can talk like that, to me!

"I'm not like you." Alton nodded in agreement. "But Paul's not like you either." *Not one little bit like you. He's caring and considerate, and you just think about yourself.*

"No need to start a debate. We don't know what they want." Mo suddenly ceased pacing and sat on one of the benches.

"Yep. If they want reading and deep thinking, Alton's probably the guy," Mark conceded.

Efficient but friendly guards called each of the teenagers in turn into a small private room where paperwork and personal details were checked. The men then awaited a welcome speech from the person in charge of their new home.

"Welcome to West Beach. I am Dr. Setchell, the governor of this adult men's unit." A short, stout lady with white hair wearing a gray suit addressed the four men. She was much older than any woman Alton had seen at The Foresters. "You will rarely see me, but I know everything that goes on. I'll be monitoring your progress."

The welcome speech, delivered in the reception area, was not warm and friendly in tone. The impersonal delivery by an officious woman suggested she had recited these words many times before.

"You are lucky to be here. Not all men get this chance, and very few men want to leave. You can enjoy a splendid life here, with luxuries and privileges not available to men anywhere else, and you can live out your entire life here. So congratulations on making it this far."

"West Beach is different from the homes you are used to at...," she paused. "The Foresters and Eb's Farm. You have to work, of course, but the work hours are short and the work itself you will find pleasant enough. I expect polite, compliant behavior as you do your duties."

Still and silent. The men forgot to breathe, so intent on discovering more about this unit.

"In return, the rewards are great, as you will see for yourself when you tour the building shortly." She steered the speech away from the nature of their work. Despite her positive words, Miss Setchell acted like she was taking delivery of a batch of chickens, not people. It did little to settle the nerves of the four teenagers in the room.

"In a few minutes, you will meet your mentors, men who have had many years of experience living here. They will show you around, and they are the first people you go to with problems or questions."

"You will also have a personal Matriarch. She is your teacher. You will see her frequently in the first few weeks. You can request to see her at any time if there are problems. The women who work here at West Beach all want to help you make a success of your life here. They're here to help."

"Now wait here for your mentors. They will answer any questions." She abruptly turned and left.

"What the?" said Mo with his arms out outstretched, palms facing upwards.

"Ferrets in feathers, was that all about?" asked Cecil, completing Mo's question.

They didn't know what they would find at West Beach and the welcome speech told them nothing that they didn't already know. It didn't tell them why they were among the chosen few or what made this place so unique.

"All sounds good to me. Just show me what I gotta do," said Mark.

His positive attitude made him so popular in his former home. Younger boys were impressed by someone who always had an opinion, or at least something to say.

Alton said nothing.

"Alton?" The head of an elderly, short black man with silvery gray hair peered around the side of a door. As four faces turned toward him, he did not wait for a reply.

"Come with me," he said, and he disappeared.

Alton picked up his bag, nodded to the others, and quickly followed through the door into West Beach Men's Unit beyond.

"I'm Max. It's my job to show you around WB and help you find your feet over the next few weeks," he said as they strolled down a long white light corridor.

With silvery hair and a deeply lined face, Mentor Max appeared to be one of the oldest men Alton had ever met and yet he walked with a spritely gate unlike the tired adults of The Foresters.

"WB? West Beach, right?"

Windows lined the corridor. To the left, they looked outside onto a swimming pool, bar, and patio area. Beyond that, Alton saw tennis courts, basketball courts, further grounds, and buildings. It was a hot morning at the end of the summer. Many of the men outside were shirtless, in just shorts—some playing sports, some sitting at tables playing games, and others lazing in loungers. A pleasant picture of tanned and toned, muscular bodies.

The pace slowed to a halt as Alton looked out of the window, mesmerized by it all. The grounds were vast, as they had been at his previous home, but the view from that building was of fields and wilderness. Now Alton looked out across ornamental gardens and land cultivated for human activities.

Outside, the men engaged in animated communications, with concentration showing on their faces. They were diverse. There were men of all ages and all skin tones. Alton could not pinpoint exactly what, but there was something unusual about the way they sat, talked, moved, their general appearance.

"It's very different from what you're used to, huh?"

"Yes. It all looks so new and big," Alton answered, with wide eyes. "The garden at Foresters was overgrown. You couldn't call it a garden; it was just outside. It was like a forest; I thought that might be the reason for its name."

On the right-hand side of the corridor, the rooms were mostly neutral, white, with minimal furniture. There was nothing to suggest what they were used for, though obviously, they might have many functions. Alton knew the unit was vast from what he had seen from the outside. The perimeter walls were clearly visible from the ship off the coast.

"I know you're nervous. You have a lifetime to enjoy here, now you've grown up."

"Nervous. Why would I be nervous? What happens here?" Alton felt terrified, even though what he saw outside was far more pleasant than anything he had known in his life. It seemed unreal. He had a horrible inkling the life of luxury was in compensation for something terrible he had yet to discover.

Perhaps he had an irrational fear of the unknown. And perhaps the biggest cause of his nerves wasn't West Beach but the prospect of a reunion with Paul after so many months.

"Sex, my boy, lots of sex." Max grinned, his dark eyes sparkling. "What happens here is plenty of food, exercise, and sport. We play games, play music, and gamble. The work we do for them matriarchs is sex."

"What?" Alton wasn't sure he had heard correctly, but Max smiled, apparently used to the surprise of new guys.

"You know what sex is, do you?"

"Yes, of course."

"They need us to make babies. We have to donate semen for them. WB is the breeding center for the future human race, but that's not all. Loads of them ladies like to have sex with men. Some of them like to watch too."

"Are you serious?"

"Don't look so shocked, Alton. They pay well. You get a cut and the rest of the profits fund the unit. Funds all the units. This is how we pay for things sent back on the ship to wherever you came from. All the luxuries are paid for by those women who want to pay to have sex with us."

"What if I can't do it?" Sex with women! It had never crossed his mind. He'd read about how reproduction happened in nature, and even among humans in bygone times, but not in this modern era of Matriarchy.

"You've been selected to come here because you can do it. You remember the doctors checking you every year and all the medication?"

"Yes."

"Well, they were checking you're free of the disease. You've been on different medication since you were a boy because they identified you as a disease-free child."

Mentor Max might have been talking about physiology; not the focus of Alton's concern.

"Why didn't they tell me? We all had medical checks, we all had medicine, every day. I thought we all had the disease."

"I don't know why. But can you imagine if they did tell you if you grew up your whole life knowing who would leave and who would stay? Wouldn't be nice for anyone, would it?"

"Are you saying every man here is fit and healthy?" Alton was perplexed.

"That's right. We're all perfect for making babies."

"Normal, like before the plague?" Alton was so shocked he didn't understand what he was asking.

"Well, I don't know about that. Most babies are still girls, so I guess we're not quite back to how we were. There's no one alive from the old days who can remember how we were, so it doesn't matter, does it? There's no one that old here. Even I'm not that old!" Max turned and waved his arm to indicate the direction of travel. "Come on. We need to go get you some new clothes first, then I'll show you your room and where you can shower."

Sex with women in this day and age!

It had never crossed Alton's mind. He knew that's how reproduction happened, in nature and even among humans in bygone times, but not in this modern era of Matriarchy.

CHAPTER THREE
Paul

Paul stirred at the sound of the opening door and through half-open eyes, he saw Zander enter cabin E12. Zander looked like he had been up for hours, his long dread-locked hair tied back, his jogging clothes drenched in sweat.

They were fortunate because currently only four men shared this new, six-berth room, sleeping in the three bunk beds.

Six months ago, Paul would have woken up in a similar dormitory, in a different men's unit, the one he had slept in all his life. Where he would look across from his bed and see the face of his best friend. They had grown up together like brothers and shared their room with several boys.

His former bedroom was already fading into a hazy memory, but only in some ways. As time passed, Paul found he thought about his best friend more than ever. He missed Alton.

In E12, they had already settled into comfortable and familiar roles. Rayfe and Zander were the seniors, having been residents of West Beach for ten years and more. At twenty-three, Jay had lived at West Beach for four years. Trying to settle in, Paul had yet to adjust. In his old home, the younger boys looked up to him as a leader. Now he was the youngest, newest, nobody in the community.

"You're all awake now? Morning." Zander glanced around the cabin.

"We don't need to get up so early 'cause at our age we don't need to work so hard to keep in shape." From the top bed, Jay threw his pillow and whacked Zander on the back of the head.

"Enjoy it while you can, young man," came the retort. Zander picked up the pillow and made as if to smother Jay on the top bunk.

From below, Paul could only imagine how that battle played out, but it concluded swiftly, and Jay was still chattering if ever one person had to have the final word.

"Now team," said Zander. "Lazing around like this won't get you to the top of the leaderboard."

"On the leaderboard at all would be a start. Though those youngsters don't stand a chance," said Rayfe.

"Don't you count on it. We are irresistible!" Paul retorted. He knew what Rayfe meant. Over the past few months, he'd learned that the older, richer clients preferred men closer to their own age rather than men in their early twenties. And Paul wasn't quite twenty yet, not for a few weeks.

"Well, get to the office and get booked up with clients! Don't let me down while you are a part of Zander's Dream Boys...!"

Again, Jay launched the pillow. At the same time, Paul rolled his eyes and heard a groan from Rayfe's direction. They all laughed; it was a joke a minute sharing with these boys.

"We're going to have to work on the E12 team name," said Rayfe.

"OK. Well, team. I've already checked the diary. I have a booking today, a repeat client, but none of you are booked. If you want to work, there is a group thing that's open, and you can sign up for that. If Zander's Dream Team is going to be top earners here, we all need to be busy satisfying those women."

"Know anything about it?" asked Rayfe, ignoring the second team name suggestion.

"Yeah, she's a regular client, a bit kinky, adventurous, and likes her fun with a group of guys; this time she's going for the under-thirties. The spaces will go fast, so if you like, I'll put your names down as I'm going back out now. What do you say?"

"Definitely yes for me. I can't go another day without," replied Jay.

"Paul?" Zander put his head down to see Paul in the bottom bunk. "Are you in?"

"Yes, put me down."

"Looks like a chance for team building," said Rayfe with a chuckle. "I'm in."

"Better than yesterday's 'everything's canceled due to protesters' session," Jay mumbled from his bunk. "Do you think there are protesters outside the building stopping our clients from getting in? Or is it a ploy to get us using those beat-off rooms?"

"I honestly don't believe they're running low on baby-making juice. They've been collecting and storing it for almost seventy years, and if they needed more of our jizz, they'd just tell us. You might not like the rooms, but we do get paid for the product of our labor."

"I suppose you're right, paid to jerk off or fuck ain't bad."

"Okay, if everyone's in, I'll get your names on the shortlist right away?"

The guys nodded.

"See you later," Zander said as he left.

Paul shut his eyes. He didn't want to stare as the other guys got out of their beds. His roommates weren't just great personalities but three lots of sexy in very masculine shapes.

Instead, he thought about his personal best at the impromptu sports event held the day before. He put up a good fight to come a respectable third in a couple of track events. The winners were a few years older and it would take at least a couple of years of hard training before he might be a serious gold medal contender.

Men at West Beach did more training and were so much fitter than those at his previous community. At The Foresters teenagers easily won all the competitions because men in their twenties were well on their way to becoming old.

"We youngsters should go to breakfast together. What do you say?" suggested Rayfe.

Using the basin in the room, the men splashed water on their faces and pulled on some casual clothes before they made their way up to the canteen in the main block.

The tables in the dining hall were set out in long bench-like formations with men eating on either side. The huge hall could seat hundreds and buzzed with low males voices. Over a thousand men lived at West Beach, but rarely would they all turn up for food at the same time, however, this morning the seats were almost all occupied and the room crowded.

The trio from E12 found free seats at the end of one table. Jay and Rayfe sat opposite each other at the very end of the row, and Paul sat next to Jay, leaving a vacant seat by Rayfe.

Before they'd had a chance to start eating, they were interrupted.

"Hi, Rayfe. Good morning Paul, Jay." Steven nodded to the men across the table and remained standing as he put his tray down in the empty space. It was quite possibly the only vacant space in the room.

Rayfe raised his eyes. "Steven. Hi, of course, you know these dudes. You know everyone."

"One of the many good things about being in menswear. I meet everyone on arrival. They all need new clothes when they get here." As he spoke, Steven looked at Paul and smiled.

A figure to the other side of Steven looked around, crossed his arms, and shook his head. The man opposite, sitting next to Paul, copied this movement. Waves of hostility flowed from the men and rippled across the table.

Steven glanced in their direction and looked a little flustered. "Let's catch up soon, Rayfe." He picked up his tray and scuttled off into the crowd, he disappeared out of sight.

"Fucking queer not welcome here," mumbled the man next to Paul.

"I don't know why he's still here," said his opposite number.

"What do you mean?" Paul butted in, his hackles rising as he detected the hatred and aggression oozing from the stranger beside him.

"You're new aren't you?" replied his neighbor. From the leathery skin and lines around his eyes, this man was much older, perhaps in his fifties.

Paul nodded. "I finished induction a couple of months ago."

"Well, I'd stay well clear of people like him. Touching other men isn't right and if that's what they want to do they've got no place living here."

The other man leaned across the table toward Paul and said, "It's normal men like us who earn the money here, men who go with women." He turned to Rayfe. "Isn't that right?"

"Technically yes, but I think Steven does his fair share of work," Rayfe replied, he focused on the food that he pushed around his plate.

"Fair share? How can he? He's not on the leaderboard."

"Neither am I." Rayfe looked up.

"Well, we both are. I don't need to remind you, Rayfe, but for the information of the new boy here I will spell it out. It's sex with women that pays for all of us to have a good life here and the biggest earners subsidize everyone else, all the men's units."

"That's all true, but we all work here. Guys do all sorts of work to keep the community going." Rayfe wasn't going to back down.

"Let's not argue. I just don't want to sit next to the creep, and he knows it." The man pushed his plate forward. "I'm done, so I'll see you around, lads."

The two men got up, picked up their empty plates and left, taking the gloomy atmosphere with them.

"Steven's all right. He was my roommate when I first came here when I was your age," said Rayfe looking at Paul. Jay tucked into his food as if he hadn't been listening.

"What happened?" Paul looked up.

"It may have been about eight or nine years ago. Basically, someone found out about Philip and Steven. You know they organize the clothing boutique for the unit, right?"

"Yes, of course, I recognized him," Paul replied. Like all new men, he must have visited menswear a few times in the early weeks to get the clothes he needed. "Found out what?"

"That they were kissing, touching each other as men and women do. Whatever."

"Whatever? Well, I'd like to know more about the whatever!" Jay chipped in with a big grin; he was listening after all.

"It wasn't funny, Jay. Steven's a nice guy, and he was a good influence in our room. A lot of men treated him badly when they didn't even know him."

"Did he ever try anything with you?" Jay's eyebrows raised.

"No, I don't think I'm his type." Rayfe laughed off the question but must have noticed Paul's serious expression.

"You don't need to worry, you know. They are okay guys, Steven and Philip. They keep themselves to themselves and even though men poke fun at them, they do a really good job here."

"I'm not worried about them, not in that way," Paul replied although he couldn't remember ever running into them around West Beach. "I'm more worried by how much those guys seem to hate them."

"They're harmless too. It just gives them something to talk about."

"But you're still friendly with Steven? It doesn't bother you if he's having sex with one of the other men?" Paul asked.

"No, why should it? Does it bother you? Either of you?"

"No. It's not a problem." Paul's answer came swift and emphatic.

"I've not thought about it, to be honest. I don't think it makes any difference to me," Jay replied. "But I can't imagine resorting to a man when there are all these women booking up to see me, almost every day. And if there's no woman around in the flesh there's always porn. And there are always the girls who want a group thing. Or the ladies who want to be watched. And..."

Rayfe held up a hand, interrupting Jay's flow. "Now I think about it, it might have been at a group thing that Philip and Steven were found out. They got a bit too amorous with each other, and that's how people found out." Rayfe and Jay laughed.

"Yes. It'd be a bit of a giveaway when they were supposed to be interested in the woman and not each other," Paul said, with a chuckle.

"Seriously, though, I think a lot of the men might be envious of them." Rayfe stared at his food.

"Envious?" questioned Jay.

"Yes, they have a relationship that doesn't rely on someone from the outside making a booking, and it doesn't involve someone having enough money to pay to see them. They even get to spend days together doing ordinary stuff."

"Rayfe, it sounds like you're the one who's envious. Have you been falling in love with the clients?" asked Jay.

Rayfe leaned across the table and whispered, "I frequently fall in love with them. When I charm them with flattering comments, I totally convince myself it's all true."

Paul and Jay chuckled.

"Seriously, I convince myself more than them!"

"With your reputation for charm, how come you're not on the leaderboard every week?"

"When you get to know who those names are you will realize that they are older guys. It is rare for anyone under thirty to get on it regularly because most of the clients are older. They will pay more to see men closer to their own age, or at least not as young as us. Guys in their thirties, forties and even fifties build up a big business of high paying repeat customers."

"We'll be all on there soon. Teamwork," said Jay.

"Yes, I'm up for that challenge!" Paul imagined the kudos of being the youngest man on the leaderboard. The guys who consistently made it into the top positions were held in high esteem and treated as heroes.

"Eat up. We've gotta check what time today's group session is and make sure Zander's got our names down," said Rayfe.

Jay held his head up in an exaggerated pose, ran one hand over his sun-kissed strawberry blonde hair and another down his chest as he spoke. "And now you know, you two better keep your hands off me if you don't want to be treated as pariahs. I've heard guys can get carried away at these group orgy things."

"Jay, much as you are totally gorgeous, I can assure you I won't get carried away," replied Paul. "What about you Rayfe, can you resist him?"

Before Rayfe answered Jay butted in: "It's you I'm particularly worried about, Paul, seeing as we share a bed. Do you know how people will talk?"

"It's a bunk bed!" *But if only you knew*, thought Paul.

"Have you guys worked together before?" asked Paul as the three of them approached the room in the main building where they were to meet the other men doing the group session.

"No," they replied in unison.

"So does this sort of thing happen often?"

"Yes," they replied again.

"We might be a team but talking with one voice is taking it a bit far," said Paul.

"Most women book a one-to-one session, of course. Sometimes they want two men, so you could say a group thing is fairly unusual. Not many women book groups of men, but the chance to work as part of a group comes along surprisingly often," Rayfe clarified.

"Yes, almost every week. And it can be good when you are new here, young, and not so much in demand," Jay added.

"I can't imagine you not being in demand, gorgeous," teased Paul. He was joking, but he meant it. He found it difficult to tear his eyes away from Jay in his presence and imagine what it would be like to run his hands over the young man's fine form.

"I know! Hard to believe I'm just an undiscovered treasure!" Jay pointed his thumbs at himself.

They arrived at room fifty-five, and the door was open. Rayfe led the way in, whispering, "Eyes off my ass boys," as Jay and Paul followed.

They paused at a check-in desk where a guard marked off their names; they were the last to arrive. They'd delayed things, messing about at Zander's pep talk, when he shared everything he knew about this particular client, her preferences, kinks and weaknesses. They ran through a mock choreography of what they might do in the session.

The guard called out for attention. "OK. Now you are all here I will tell you what is expected. This is a bit unusual. Your client is behind a one-way mirror in the next room. You are going to go in one at a time and perform for her, she will be able to see you, but you can't see her. She might speak to you, and she can hear whatever you say. She is going to choose a few of you to meet her in person, but she wants to be able to choose you based on how you perform in the audition. Everyone here gets paid for the audition, but the big money goes to those who are selected to spend the whole session with her."

The room erupted with chatter and grumbles, almost every man wanted to ask a question.

"What do you mean, perform? What sort of thing does she want us to do?"

The Dream Team stayed calm. Without saying a word they nodded to each other and Jay could not resist a prayer entitled, *Thank you, Zander.*

The client was a regular at West Beach. None of these younger men had ever seen her, but she was well known to the older men. Zander had told his roommates all about her likes and dislikes. They had no idea they would be in competition for her attention, but they were well prepared for this.

"We'll do what we did back in the room earlier and mention each other's names too, right?" asked Rayfe.

"Right," said Paul.

"And we thought we were mucking about," added Jay. "We'll tell her we work together as the Dream Team."

"Good."

The guard banged on the table to draw everyone's attention. "The only fair way to do this is if I pull your names out of a hat. I've already done that and got a random list here. Rayfe you're first. Just go into the next room and when you've finished come back in here."

Eventually, Paul's turn came, and he ran his fingers through his hair as he exited through the door. He took a deep breath, relaxed, and strolled into the adjacent room. He strode confidently into the middle of the space and stood still, posing as if he were modeling clothes.

He fixed his gaze straight ahead and hoped he was looking her in the eye though he had no idea of her location behind the one-way glass. He took his time, to let her know in this audition that he lacked nervousness, with no fumbling and hurried gestures. His self-confidence should appeal to her.

"My name is Paul; I'm here today with two friends, Rayfe and Jay. We call ourselves the Dream Team because we work well together. If you like what you see and want to see a whole lot more, you know who to ask for. Mention all our names and you won't be disappointed."

He turned and walked out without looking back.

That was it. Minimal. Confident.

The performance presented exactly as they had rehearsed in their room.

Zander had told them this woman likes confident men who keep their clothes on for a long time. She enjoys the mystery and the tease.

Performance over, Paul returned to the waiting room. The team delighted in seeing how anxious the other men were as each wondered what they might do to attract her favor. Despite not knowing his roommates too well, Paul was sure Jay and Rayfe would do something similar to him.

Although he was also willing to bet Jay spoke a lot more.

Jay would never stick to one sentence if three or four might convey the same message.

"Just a few more minutes and we'll know if we've got the night off," said Jay when the final person returned.

"Do I have your attention?" Quiet fell over the room. "Rayfe, Jay, Paul, proceed to room forty-five, please."

Without waiting to listen to the complaints of those not chosen, the three men crashed as they tried to pass through the door at the same time, then they raced the short distance along the corridor to room forty-five.

Rayfe said, "We haven't discussed what we'll do next. I think we should enter and keep in the same characters that we rehearsed because those are the guys she chose."

Jay winked at Paul. "And anything that goes on in these rooms is confidential, right?"

"That's right," replied Rayfe, and he knocked on the door.

Paul gulped; it was as if Jay read his mind.

CHAPTER FOUR
Alton

Max stopped at a door. Taking up a position outside, he signaled Alton to enter.

Alton entered what seemed like a vast storeroom. With shelves from floor to ceiling filled with Alton wasn't sure what.

"Hello handsome," said the man who stood just inside the room. "Don't tell me, I know it's your first day. You've just arrived, and I have your name on my notepad here. So which one are you?" He tapped the pad on the table beside him.

"I'm Alton." He peered over and pointed to the top name on the list. "That's me."

"Pleased to meet you. I'm Philip, and over there is my partner in crime Steven." He gestured dramatically in the direction of a man sitting at a sewing machine, at the far end of the room. Steven gave a small wave. "We call ourselves the Wardrobe Masters. There's nothing we can't do with fabrics. Well, that's another story. If you need something amazing, something unusual, perhaps a costume—if it can be made with a sewing machine, darling, you know where to come."

Alton smiled, enjoying Philip's passionate enthusiasm for his work.

"Now I need you to stand like a bird. Arms out so I can measure you."

Philip flitted around with his tape measure. On a fresh page of his notepad he jotted down details, uttering words aloud to himself. "Arm length, collar, chest, waist."

"Just the inside leg still to do. You hold this end at the top, deary." He handed one end of the tape measure to a perplexed looking Alton. "Just next to the naughty bits, not too close."

Philip got down on his knees to check the bottom of the tape measure.

"And, okay, job done."

"I've never been measured for clothes before."

"No, a lot of the boys who arrive here have never worn new clothes before."

"I don't think I've ever been the first in my clothes, someone older has always worn them before me," Alton said. Many of those hand-me-downs came from his slightly older and taller best friend; he liked wearing clothes that had once wrapped around Paul's body.

"Now you're here, that's all going to change. Steven and I are going to make sure you look good enough to eat," Philip said, sounding like he meant it.

"I won't argue with that." Alton enjoyed the energy in the room, and he wanted to be a part of it. "Make me look delicious and I'll let you have a nibble."

"Just a nibble? I might get greedy and gobble you all up."

"Stop the flirting and give the boy some clothes," Steven called from behind his sewing machine and Philip started moving around the room and through a door into what appeared to be a stock room. "Don't encourage him; he gets over-excited when there are new arrivals."

"Sorry, sir."

"No need to be sorry, I'm just trying to help you. Philip will keep you here chatting for hours."

Philip returned with a small pile of clothes that he dropped into Alton's arms.

"He's helping you get out of here. He knows I'd keep you talking all day. And, of course, you are welcome to stay and socialize with us anytime." Waving a hand over the pile of clothing, he continued, "This is just basic stuff so you've got something to wear. Come back later today, after you've showered, and you can choose some more and try it on here. I'll sort out new shoes for you then as well."

"Why didn't you come in too?" Alton asked when he rejoined Max outside.

"I don't like to go in there unless I have to." Without making eye contact, Max had already started walking toward a large wide staircase. "I don't like the smell in there."

Alton followed as they climbed the stairs. His head buzzed, processing the new information and dismissing the comment about the smell as just a little strange.

Women. He'd given them so little thought, as they figured so little in his life. The guards were all women. But he'd given no consideration to the process of human reproduction and whether he might ever be required to participate.

"All new recruits sleep in the chambers along this corridor. This is yours, son." Max stopped at the open door. "It's tiny, but you and other new recruits only sleep in here." The dormitory had six bunk beds tightly packed together. Two chairs, one table, two small cupboards, and insufficient empty floor space for a group of men to stand.

"A friend came here about six months ago; it would be good to share with him."

"Changing rooms shouldn't be a problem, there's plenty of space in other rooms, but this is where you stay when you first arrive while you find your feet and do your training. What's his name?"

"Paul Knight."

"No." Max shook his head. "I can't place the name but if he's here, we'll run into him soon."

Alton had the communal shower room to himself. Having been in the same clothes for the whole journey, he was glad to get out of them. It seemed like forever since he'd been clean. The powerful jets of water and soap also refreshed him after many restless nights.

His encounter with the Wardrobe Masters had also made him aware of his shabby appearance. Something he took for granted at Foresters, as all the clothes that everyone wore appeared almost as old as the buildings, which themselves dated back to pre-Matriarchy. He realized that one of the striking differences between the men back home and here was how well-dressed they were.

And there was something else that Alton couldn't quite identify.

Thinking about the men he'd seen through the windows aroused more than just thoughts. This was not the time to have a hard-on, not in a communal shower room when anyone could walk in. He forced his mind to focus on his anxieties about the place and tempered his libido.

When Alton returned to his room, he felt like a new man. Clean. His shaggy blond hair still wet and dripping on the new baby-blue T-shirt, which hung over new jeans. He'd never been so smart.

"That's better," Max said, who had waited for him the whole time.

"The Wardrobe Master said I should go back after my shower."

"Don't worry, I'll take you there later today. They need to get clothes for all you new boys. And now they've seen you, they'll have a pile of stuff ready and waiting if we give 'em time."

"Oh right." Alton felt almost disappointed. He looked forward to going back to that friendly oasis in this scary place.

"I'll take you on more of a tour, and then we'll stop by the canteen, for late breakfast or early lunch. We might see your friend Paul there before the afternoon show. Oh, I should have asked, did they give you breakfast?"

At the mention of food, Alton realized how hungry he was. There were snacks available on arrival, but he had been too anxious to eat. None of the new recruits ate anything.

"I could do with food. What's the afternoon show?"

"It's an excellent introduction to what goes on here, where you can just watch, and you don't have to do anything. Let's go."

It sounded ominous.

After a brief tour taking in some parts of the building and vast grounds, they headed back to the canteen in the main building. As they entered the double doors, they almost crashed into a man exiting from the dining hall.

The dining room was full of men queuing with trays in their hands, selecting food from a self-service counter, and sitting at utilitarian tables and chairs. It was noisy with the sound of metal cutlery, glass, and crockery clattering together, and a low-pitched hum of male voices.

At a glance, there appeared to be more than a hundred men in the room. A complete cross-section of age, ethnicity, and height. Alton scanned the room for a familiar face that he didn't find. He was ravenous but that might not have been the cause of the pains in his stomach, and he doubted whether he'd be able to eat.

West Beach was a very bizarre world.

At The Foresters, boys grew up as part of a large caring family of asexual men. Today, Alton discovered thriving sexuality right here near the Capital.

His excitement at the prospect of an imminent reunion with Paul was dwarfed by fear of his new home, whether he could make his way in this place, make this work, do the work. In view of all he was discovering about this world at WB, Alton feared just how that reunion meeting would go.

As they ate, Max gave him a rundown of the induction process.

"Tomorrow you will meet Walsh. She will train you. You'd think sex would be natural, and it is, but they want to teach you how to do it right so you give maximum pleasure to the customers."

"How do they teach it?"

"Some women volunteer to go with the new boys during the training."

Alton must have looked totally not thrilled by this prospect.

"You don't need to worry, they are very relaxed and friendly."

"What if I don't want to have sex with a woman?"

"You'll love it. You don't need to worry about that," Max chuckled.

Alton wasn't so sure.

After they'd finished eating, Max announced it was time to prepare for the afternoon show.

"I'm going to introduce you to sex," said Max.

The first few days slipped by surprisingly fast. The trainers had organized an intensive induction program. Activities and new information filled every waking moment. Exhausting but not unpleasant days unfolded for the new arrivals.

The four new recruits stayed together for most of the time, along with at least one mentor. Physical Exercise, Intellectual Pursuits, and the Sex Training sessions took up most of the time. Otherwise known as PE, IP, and ST.

Structured activities left little spare time for socializing with the other men. Card games and gambling were popular pastimes at WB according to the mentors, but the new recruits had no time for these activities through the first week of induction.

Sex Training, it turned out was only a minor part of the preparation for working at West Beach. Looking good and being able to hold an intelligent conversation were as important to women as any sexual prowess. The trainers also coached the men in social skills, sessions jokingly tagged as Charm School.

PE consisted of running, swimming, weight training and sports such as tennis and basketball. All were optional, to a point, though physical exercise in one form or another was compulsory.

Alton had no hesitation in maximizing his time in the gym lifting the weights. He had bulked up considerably over the last year or so, always pushing himself at manual tasks on the farm. He had volunteered for the hard work to ensure that he went to sleep exhausted. The increased size of his muscles was a welcome side effect. He remembered Paul admiring his well-developed physique on more than one occasion.

Within a few days, Alton discovered the bodybuilding fraternity who spent a lot of time in the gym working on their impressive sculptured bodies. Individuals gave him tips but also showed him the section of the library dedicated to information on bodybuilding as well as books on general health, fitness, and nutrition.

"Be careful you don't overdo it, though. You have to keep in mind what the clients want," Cray warned him.

Cray was one of the fitness instructors who ran the gym. He had the body of a Greek god, due to hours spent working out, but because he followed his own advice, he was not as large as the men in the specialist bodybuilding books.

"Women like a strong, muscular man but when you start looking like the fellas in these books you reduce the potential market for your body," Mat said.

"That's right," agreed Tom. "Most women don't want a man who looks like that. He'd be a niche commodity."

"Niche isn't all bad, who wants to be average?" Rod was one of the more pumped up of the weight addicts. He may well have had the biggest biceps at WB.

"Niche can be good, of course, if you like those clients and if there are enough of them," said Cray.

"And bad if there are too many fish in the small pond. He's right. It is a small pond with not many ladies fishing in it. So you do us both a favor and don't try to get guns as big as these." Rod's arms were the size of tree trunks.

"Average is really good then?" asked Alton. "Lots fishing in that lake?"

"Average is not for you, boy," Rod replied. "You ain't average. You're about average height but even the first day you came in here you were all pumped up as if you've been working out wherever it is you came from. I'd recommend you aim to maintain that size, don't get no bigger, but don't aim for average."

One day the gym session turned out to be something very different, not PE.

"We're not doing exercise this morning, we're going to be looking at massage."

Cray led the trainees through a side door, which looked like it would lead to a cupboard, but actually took them into a tiny vestibule with further doors through to a series of small massage rooms. Each was completely equipped with oil, towels, and equipment around the massage bed, which took up most of the room.

"A few of us have trained in massage and anatomy so we can look after your sports injuries, for example."

"You will not be expected to give the ladies professional massages. If they wanted to, they would go to a masseuse. Nevertheless, it is useful to know how to give a basic massage. Your clients may be stressed or nervous, and this can help to relax them. It is also something you can practice with each other. Although you might also practice this with the ladies in your ST sessions."

The boys took it in turns to lie on the table and to try out techniques supervised by Cray. It was far from a relaxing massage session though. With many people crowded into the small room talking, and with so many hands on each body, it became obvious that the boys had no idea what a massage involved.

"I would suggest you all come for more training, perhaps just in twos. This is a useful skill to be able to pull out of the bag when you get stuck in a room with a client and things are not going well."

Intellectual Pursuits to stimulate the mind took many forms, from reading and structured debates to board games, chess, and playing cards.

"Why were we taking daily medication before we came here and not now?" asked Alton in the IP session run by Mark's mentor, Chas. He'd asked for discussion topics, and the only things running through Alton's mind related to his past; he decided to go with this one.

"Who knows?" Mo shrugged his shoulders. "How can we answer that?"

"Who cares!" said Mark. He clearly didn't but if he hoped for the support of his apathy, he didn't get it.

"It's a topic we can discuss even if we don't know the answer. That is the point of these sessions, not to find answers but to stimulate intellectual curiosity and practice discussion." Chas took the suggestion seriously. "What do you think, Alton?"

"I don't know how it works at other units, but at ours, we were told we had to have treatment for the disease and it was related to the plague. We all have the disease; we were born with it."

"Same at Eb's," Cecil agreed.

"No mystery is there? We're not ill so we don't need medicine. Otherwise, we wouldn't be here." Mark slouched further back in his chair, apparently bored by the subject. Bored by any subject raised by Alton.

"We had medication right up to the day we left. They must've known we were cured before then." Alton thought about his conversation with Barb on the morning of the announcement. She had been in charge of the morning meds for a whole year, and she seemed to know Alton was leaving with her. How long had she known? How had she known? "Max said we were free of disease since we were kids, so was it covered up?"

All eyes went toward Chas, the only mentor present in this session.

"I don't know. Max might know more about it than me." Chas looked perplexed and scratched his head. "Sounds like he made up that story."

"Alton's got a point," said Cecil. "It's all strange."

Alton wondered about how, on the whole, the men here were not just fitter and more alert than at The Foresters but also seemed to have a mental superiority. Was it a coincidence? Were they naturally that way? Was that why they were selected for transfer? Or was it a consequence of how they spent their time, in stimulating activities.

What role, if any, did the meds play?

Alton dreaded ST, which took place daily. It usually turned out to be not quite as bad as he feared, but it was never something he enjoyed.

The first session was a biology lesson involving all four boys in a classroom with textbooks. The next day they split up to work privately. They each met their personal Matriarchs, a different woman for each man, who would be their ST tutors.

Alton's Matriarch was a middle-aged woman called Walsh.

Walsh explained that personal Matriarchs had a broad remit. She handled an individual's welfare and had his best interests at heart. Apparently, this meant helping him to be good at his job, satisfying clients, and earning money. If the men were earning, the unit did too. The men individually always got a percentage of the money spent by the customers.

The second and subsequent sex lessons in the first week were on an individual basis. Alton met his Matriarch, Walsh outside of their allocated room, and together they entered.

"This is Freya, she's a volunteer here, and she's happy for you to practice with her."

"Hello Freya," said Alton, racked with nerves and dread.

"Hi." She smiled, without a sign of self-consciousness even though she sat on a bed wearing nothing but cream-colored lace panties.

Freya looked fragile. Her petite body was reminiscent of the younger, prepubescent boys back home. Boys whose lips curled when they hurt themselves and they tried to fight back tears. *Boys.*

Alton's every instinct was to look out for the younger boys and keep them from harm. Their scrawny limbs looked like they could snap. He recoiled at the sight of the waif-like figure presented to him as a possible sexual partner but tried to show nothing to the two pairs of eyes watching him.

Her smile was warm and welcoming. She patted the bed indicating for Alton to sit next to her, but she didn't speak. Alton didn't move toward the girl but remained frozen near the entrance, assessing the situation in front of him.

Freya's delicate face was surrounded by long, fine hair tumbling down over slender shoulders. Freya may well have been eighteen, nineteen, or in her early twenties and closer in age to him than most of the women he had ever previously encountered.

To date, he had only met guards and Walsh. They always seemed so old, so distant and so different.

Walsh broke the silence. "Don't be nervous, you don't have to do anything if you don't want to, but I would strongly encourage you to have a go. Everything we do and say in this room is confidential. Freya and I won't tell anybody else about what takes place, so there is no need to feel shy or embarrassed."

Walsh was more mature and more sturdy. She looked more like the women Alton was used to seeing, more like the guards. She wore a similar style of clothing to the guards but in black. Black, trousers, big boots, and a baggy cotton top.

"Freya is a volunteer, and she is going to be your training partner," said Walsh. "Every man progresses at a different pace, but I want to explain these sessions are not about learning to have sex. They are about learning to satisfy our female customers in a physical way. So it is about sex and sensuality. It is about knowing how to touch a lady all over, to read her body language and do or say the right thing to her at the right time."

In the first session Freya masturbated, Walsh talked, and an embarrassed but curious Alton watched. Despite being urged to put his fingers in and being assured that nothing would hurt him, Alton touched the woman as if touching a naked flame, pulling his hands back quickly so as to not get burned.

Alton dreaded returning to ST the following day, but it turned out to be quite pleasant. Again Freya wore panties when he entered the room. This time, he gave her a sensual back massage, and Freya and Walsh gave him feedback.

Initially, her body seemed so slight in his hands. He concentrated. He knew what it felt like to care for someone, and he channeled those sincere feelings, wanting her to experience that through the touch of his hands.

Walsh and Freya both agreed he had a natural aptitude for sensual touch and urged him to continue to her legs and then the rest of her body.

"You can remove Freya's panties if you want to but you don't have to go that far today."

He didn't want to.

Walsh reassured him that lots of men reacted like this at first because interactions with women were unusual. Listening to the bravado of the other men; however, Alton suspected his repulsion was unusual.

He did not dislike Freya, she seemed very pleasant, but he had no desire to touch her. Talking to her, on the other hand, was fascinating. In charge of the sessions, Walsh encouraged wide-ranging conversation when physical contact seemed destined to fail. Talking might break down the barriers that built up over years of not mixing with women. She suggested Alton might just need to get to know a woman better, to build up his confidence in female company.

The leaderboard listing the top earners acted as a prime motivator as well as a source of entertainment. Positioned in a high visibility location in the canteen, it provided a focus for speculation, bragging, and gambling. Updated weekly, it gave all men an incentive to work hard. If the work itself didn't motivate a man to put on his best show for the clients, then the competitive instinct might move him.

Being on that board provided a way of boasting to your peers without having to say anything. In fact, big-mouthed boasters might be liars whereas the board confirmed the identities of the busiest, best-paid men. therefore the most popular workers in the unit. Giving a great service could lead to repeat bookings, for example, which automatically helped in the leaderboard rankings.

The top men were the best at their job and the biggest earners.

All men benefited from that income, as a proportion of it subsidized not just West Beach but all the other male communities across the land. So, whether it was a matter of doing good for the community, healthy competition, or self-respect, all men had great incentive to appear on that board.

In ST, the women explained that sex benefited humanity, by providing a service that made people feel good and, at the same time, transferring resources from the Capital populated by women to the poor male communities. West Beach and all the men's units benefited from the money spend by lusty women seeking male prostitutes. As if altruism provided a greater motivation for some men to do this work rather than personal pleasure and lust.

When the new recruits were alone, they didn't talk about the greater good, or about their roles as paid workers. The young men's exchanges were about fucking women because they liked it.

Alton didn't join in. He couldn't.

In a new environment, with new people, learning and doing new things Alton spent much of the first week feeling stressed and exhausted. He became increasingly concerned that he couldn't do what needed to be done to work here even though Walsh seemed unworried.

Another day without seeing Paul, Alton thought each night as he lay in his bunk in the tiny cramped room, torturing himself with *what ifs*. Alton shuddered as an unwanted thought seized him, the same thought every day.

Paul is working. Now he has sex with women.

How much will he have changed? Has the work changed him?

There was only so long that two men could avoid each other even in a men's unit the size of a small town, like West Beach.

Alton wanted to see Paul, but would he have the nerve to tell him what he should have told him when they were both home at The Foresters? Perhaps it didn't even matter now.

It had to happen. Inevitably.

The trainees were heading toward lunch. Well aware of the high traffic volumes through those busy doors, having witnessed a number of close encounters, Alton entered with caution to avoid a collision.

"Paul!" Alton stopped suddenly, causing Max to crash into him. The rest of the team wandered past unaware that Alton had come to a halt causing a blockage amidst the free flow of traffic and not hearing his whispered exclamation.

Paul stood still, his eyes wide and his mouth open, frozen in surprise.

"No need to look so pleased," mumbled Alton, not sure what reaction either of them should have had at that moment. In a crowded public place and blocking the flow of traffic to and from the dining room.

"I am pleased. It's just..." Paul spoke quietly and shifted about, moving his weight from foot to foot. He looked at Max as if to ask how much Alton had already been told. "I've got to go to work so we'll catch up later."

"Yes, later." Alton's insides twisted in knots as Paul moved to walk past them. Apparently, Paul couldn't get away fast enough, but then he stopped, put his hand on Alton's arm, and said in a barely audible whisper, "I am really pleased."

He's really pleased.

Briefly, Alton's insides jumped for joy.

Paul had hurried away all too quickly and to what? To work.

Alton could still feel the place on his arm where Paul's hand rested and Paul's breath against his ear as he whispered.

CHAPTER FIVE
Paul

Seeing Alton in the canteen was a shock.

Crashing into Alton shook Paul up. And when what happened really sunk in, he was disappointed by how he'd handled the reunion. He should have prepared for that, he was aware he might meet Alton again one day.

He should have been ready because he'd hoped he would see Alton at WB.

Ashamed at how he'd handled the reunion, he beat a hasty retreat to his bedroom—the mention of work a mere excuse to escape. He kicked off his shoes and lay down on his bottom bunk, the only place he could think of to escape for quiet and privacy in the afternoon. His roommates were unlikely to disturb him for a few hours and if someone did enter, he'd just claim a headache.

He regretted running off, but what could he have done differently?

He should have been ready with welcoming and reassuring words. He remembered his terrifying first week at WB. The sense of an alien home-work environment overwhelming him.

Alton had looked scared and bewildered; Paul recalled feeling just the same when he'd arrived here months earlier.

He wished he'd been able to reassure his friend by saying something helpful.

Having started with a lie as a way of escaping from the uncomfortable situation quickly, Paul needed to lie low so as not to run into Alton again too soon.

The work! What would Alton think of the work?

In fact, Paul probably did have a headache.

Despite their history, Paul had spent the past few months at WB trying to put all thoughts of Alton out of his mind including the painful memory of parting. At first he reassured himself that the younger man would soon follow. With sadness, over time he acknowledged they might never meet again. Most men weren't transferred to West Beach.

The old feelings were just as strong. He craved Alton's companionship. The man was fun to be with and a good friend. A quiet but strong personality that Paul found so attractive. Paul just needed some time alone to reflect on the changed situation and figure out what to do next.

Paul had changed a lot over the past few months, and he knew Alton must have changed too.

He replayed the brief incident over and over in his mind. Alton looked the same as always. Messy blond hair that needed a cut. A little bit older and bigger. Alton had always been the short, stocky one, but he seemed broader, more muscled. He drew in a deep breath, remembering touching Alton's arm. The familiar gray eyes looking at him. Standing close enough to smell him. Close enough to kiss him. Even though he didn't, he wanted to.

Paul moved his hand to his swelling cock, an automatic reaction, alone in the privacy of his room. Erections he had with his dreams of Alton were different from those he had with clients; he yearned for Alton with his whole body.

Paul hastily pushed down his trousers, kicking them onto the floor. Alone with his hand, comfortable on his bed, overwhelmed by thoughts of Alton. His broad shoulders, his smile, his scent. More erotic fantasies replaced the recollection of touching him so briefly in the food hall and being close enough to smell him. He could imagine him, imagine licking his skin, biting him, tasting him. A very different outcome from their encounter.

Paul grabbed some tissue to clean himself up with a new resolve to make amends.

Early in the morning, Paul rose as soon as Zander left for his pre-dawn run. The grounds extended over many acres and most of the men ran daily. They were exceptionally fit, in contrast to grown men at the Foresters.

Early in the morning was a good time to seek some solitude and avoid the heat of the end of the still hot days at the end of summer.

Alton lived at West Beach!

That fact played on Paul's mind almost continuously and he figured that the longer he left things, the worse it would be. He wanted to speak to his old friend. Hoping to grab Alton before the day got underway, he loitered in the corridor above the office, upstairs in the main building, where the new recruits were billeted.

Paul knew the intensive induction left little time for the new trainees to integrate with the rest of West Beach's residents in the first few weeks, so Paul realized just hoping to stumble across each other was leaving too much to chance if he wanted to meet up with Alton soon.

There was little to look at in the main corridors of the vast, modern main building. Surrounded by gleaming white walls and closed doors Paul took up a station midway along the corridor, next to the bathrooms. He slumped to the floor, prepared to be there for quite a while.

Paul felt guilty. He remembered how difficulty he had adjusting to life at WB, the great culture shock. He believed he should have been a better source of support for Alton in his first week and hoped to make amends.

As a human ball of mixed emotion, Paul became increasingly uncomfortable, alone on the floor in the quiet corridor. He sat near the central stairwell and only one floor above the hub of operations: the booking office next to the dining hall. Two of the busiest places in the community visited by all the residents several times daily. He heard movement in the building. West Beach never slept.

Paul remained on the floor undisturbed for many minutes and lost track of time while pondering what he might say. He came up with nothing. Good friends, they once were but stalking his prey in the early morning might come across as weird. Desperate, and not in a good way.

What would he say?

Paul made a dash for the stairs, regretting this expedition, and raced down them to avoid being caught and looking like an idiot.

"Paul, what are you doing here?" The familiar voice came from in front and not behind as feared.

Zander paused, waiting for Paul to descend the last few steps. As a major thoroughfare, the corridor was larger than many of the rooms in the building. A steady trickle of bleary-eyed people meandered through, paying no attention to each other.

"Morning. I'm thinking of canceling today's client." Why had he blurted that out? Excuses weren't needed.

Zander's eyebrows raised. "You're up early if you're not feeling well," he said.

"I feel fine. I just don't like seeing her." Anxiety coiled inside the pit of Paul's stomach, maybe he had steered the conversation in the wrong direction. He spoke the truth, but perhaps illness was a more acceptable reason for canceling a client.

Zander's eyes grew wider. An unspoken question on his face or perhaps disbelief?

Irrational guilt clouded Paul's thought process. "I've never canceled anybody before."

"It's up to you. You don't have to see any woman you don't like."

Maybe just imagination, paranoia, but Paul sensed a big question mark behind the statement.

"That's what people say," said Paul. "It seems a bit odd not to go ahead. Like I should have an explanation, but I don't have a good reason to cancel."

"OK, I'll bite. Why don't you want to see her?" asked Zander.

"Too intense. She's too intense. As if she thinks she means something more to me; more than just a client for the hour. I find it draining, acting as her boyfriend. It's not like that with other clients but this one. She has unreal expectations." Concerns about what to say to Alton slipped from his mind as new concerns about what to say to his high maintenance client replaced them.

"Cancel and you don't tell her anything. The matriarchs liaise with the clients." Zander turned toward the office as if the conversation were over.

"Wouldn't be so bad if it was just an hour. She's here every week, for lengthy sessions. Dinner and conversation."

That got Zander's attention. He stood still and turned to look at Paul. "No one ditches regulars. Who is it?"

"Kerry Thompson. She doesn't get her role as just a client." Kerry came as a WB gold client, the desired prize for most workers, not one to casually discard.

"I see." Zander paused, but he hadn't finished as he raised his hands in preparation for his next words.

"As your friend, I must point out that every man wants a bunch of clients like her to make life easy. Kerry is one of the best clients to have as a regular because she's a big-money item. She's earned her gold membership card here. Not many women can afford to visit us as often or for longer sessions like she can. In the best rooms too. Clients like her take you closer to becoming a permanent figure on the leaderboard. You should make the most of it."

Paul resisted the temptation to start with a whining *but*. "Rayfe makes the acting sound easy. *'Flatter them and charm them'* he says, and if it were less frequent, it wouldn't be so difficult. I find it awkward."

"But she books more often, too often." Zander finished the thought. "It isn't always easy. Paul, just do it for the reward. Walsh said our roommates should all be on the leaderboard so don't let us down. Just cancel today. Say you're ill and prepare for next time. See Walsh for some coping tips."

CHAPTER SIX
Alton

Since arriving at West Beach, Alton had been almost continuously in the company of the other trainees and their teachers, and the Matriarchs or the mentors. The relentless induction timetable allowed little time for idle socializing.

They were cocooned away from most of the men at West Beach. Alton saw them in the very busy canteen at mealtimes, as he walked along the corridors, the endless maze of corridors, and as they participated in sports indoors and out. It was a lively place. People were always milling about and even when they were sitting around they were never doing nothing.

For many hours in the day, a band performed live music in a recreation area located in a sheltered spot outdoors, just outside the dining room. Alton wondered what happened in bad wintry weather. There was evidence of a temporary covering that could be used but perhaps they didn't get so much bad weather this far south.

At The Foresters life virtually stopped in the winter due to lack of light and warmth provided only by open fires. Technology was in evidence throughout West Beach, with solar panels across every roof and wind turbines too.

In the same area, people sat around playing card games characterized by animated activity and concentration, such a contrast to downtime at The Foresters. The older men, the elders, and the grown-ups, lounged in what they called quiet contemplation. Alton called it sleeping. Like their get up and go had got up and gone; they'd almost lost the will to live; living was just about surviving.

No wonder he hadn't seen Paul sooner.

As he lay in bed, in quiet contemplation, reflecting on the differences between his two homes and the chance meeting with Paul the previous day, Alton felt compelled to get up early. It may have been a sixth sense, but he imagined Paul very near, perhaps outside the door.

He sprang out of bed and opened the door and looked at the empty corridor. As if, like a hunter, he could sniff out a trail of lingering scent and he felt compelled to investigate.

Pulling on a sweater to fight the early morning chill he wandered toward the central staircase, with bare feet, and in sweatpants. Which way? He heard voices at the bottom of the stairs. Quietly he tiptoed down in time to see Paul entering the office, deep in conversation with another man. He'd have to reemerge, so Alton waited.

After only a few minutes both men appeared, still talking.

"Paul!" He'd given no thought to what would follow.

Paul and his companion turned.

"Alton!" The dilated pupils and the smile on his face showed Paul was pleased to see him, and Alton could breathe again.

"This is Zander; meet Alton. My best friend from back home." Paul made the introductions.

"Good to meet you, Alton." Zander, possibly the tallest man he'd ever seen, held out his hand. With a firm handshake that signaled both hello and goodbye, Zander said, "I expect you two'd like to catch up, and I gotta go. Talk to you later."

Zander sauntered away. Paul and Alton watched him go. They were finally alone. Sort of. They stood together on the main stairwell, not far from the dining room, just before breakfast. Individuals trailed past, most not even seeming to notice the men standing stationary.

"When did you arrive?" Paul asked.

"A few days ago, I think. It's been a blur." Alton threaded his fingers together, unsure what to do with his body.

"I remember that. How's life back home?"

"Same. Except a whole lot quieter now I should think. As Mark came here with me." They grinned. Paul understood the comment about Mark and didn't need to ask more.

They stood bashfully looking at each other for what seemed like minutes but could have only been seconds. A few people walked past, heading toward the food attraction.

When the hallway cleared, Alton said, "I've missed you," Blurting the words out quickly, fearing the opportunity might disappear as suddenly as it had arisen.

"Let's go and talk." Paul took Alton at the elbow, guiding him toward one of the many corridors that terminated there, leading into the depths of the building. "Everyone will be heading this way for breakfast," he said and let go of Alton's arm as they entered one of the passages.

"Where are we going?" asked Alton. He had learned enough of the layout to know it was a labyrinth.

"I don't know," replied Paul. "You mean you've not got a plan." And he gave him a friendly shove.

Alton pushed him back. "I might have a plan. But I don't know where we're going."

They walked at a quick pace, leaving one wing of the building and entering another.

"This way." Paul took Alton's hand and pulled him sideways into an alcove off the corridor.

Alton's heart jumped in his chest at this longed-for physical contact, but he was more surprised to see the foot of a winding staircase hidden from the view of the main corridor.

Paul kept a firm grip on Alton's hand as he led him up the spiraling stairs until they arrived back on the same floor as Alton's room but in a different part of the building. It looked older, shabby and smaller in scale than what they had left downstairs.

Partly wondering about his new surroundings, most of Alton's attention focused on his hand, the one still held by Paul.

"What's up here?" Alton's voice came out as a whisper.

"Offices and stuff, I don't know. Mostly used by the guards and Matriarchs. That's why it's quiet."

"No one sleeps in this area?"

"No."

As they spoke, Paul continued to lead Alton to an unknown destination.

He stopped abruptly.

They stood at the opening of a dim, narrow passage that had several doors along one side and led to a dead end.

"Have you seen down here?" asked Paul.

"I don't think so. I don't recall coming around here at all."

"They will show you soon. Come on." Paul nodded his head in the direction they were to go and added, "Stick with me for the advanced tour." Paul let go of Alton's hand to lead the way along the narrow passage. Its width determined they had to move in single file.

The doors had green 'vacant' signs by the handles. Like bathroom doors, presumably, they changed to red when occupied. Alton wondered if this was a toilet or shower block.

When they arrived outside the final door, Paul opened it and said. "You've got to see this." He stepped aside for Alton to enter.

Alton stepped in and Paul followed, flicking a switch to turn on a dim overhead light that barely cast any illumination.

The square room measured approximately three feet by three feet. A built-in padded box-seat, covered by cream leather-look upholstery took up almost half the space. Attached to the side wall, a rack held a pile of beakers, some tissues, and some magazines.

"This is what you call a box room," said Alton.

"It's called a beat off room, actually," Paul said without further explanation as he followed Alton in. Squeezing close and Alton heard the door click shut behind them.

Too aware of standing with Paul in this cramped space, Alton couldn't begin to think about the strange name or purpose of the room. Or why Paul had brought him here? Paul's hand was on Alton's back, Paul's warm body pushed close behind.

Alton wanted to turn around, and speak, face to face, but the close proximity stopped his brain from working with words, and to turn would reveal the tent that had formed so suddenly in the front of his sweatpants. Instead, he leaned back against Paul.

"I've missed you, Paul," he whispered.

With surprise, Paul's breath and lips touch his ear.

"Missed you too." Not exactly words but slight sounds on the breath that tickled his neck as the taller man leaned forward over his shoulder.

Hands moved around Alton's body. Arms embraced him. He wanted this moment to last but feared he'd somehow misread the signs and any time Paul would... what? Reject him for having an erection? It wasn't likely; perhaps he'd just laugh with him and tell him he should save it for the ladies at West Beach.

There was no mistaking it. With the lightest touch, lips brushed his ear, his neck and then his cheek. Sparks of electricity charged through his body. Kisses and caresses banished fears and doubts. Paul held Alton firmly, and his body pushed against Alton's back, he could feel Paul's arousal.

A hot tongue on his neck and the scrape of teeth gently nibbling at the sensitive flesh froze Alton to the spot, arms hanging at his side, barely daring to breathe.

Initially, Paul's hands rested on the flat of Alton's stomach, but slowly they moved in opposite directions up and down his body. Even the lightest touch over the top of clothing, over Alton's bulging crotch and sensitive nipple, caused sensations of unimaginable pleasure to surge through him.

"Turn around." The whispered words mingled with kisses on Alton's neck.

He turned and looked up toward Paul, reaching out to hold him.

Paul moved a hand to cradle the back of Alton's head bringing him closer. Their mouths met, playfully sucking and nibbling. Tongues danced together and explored leading to a deep and passionate kiss. Paul tasted familiar, of home, as if their mouths were meant to be joined and it went against nature for them to be apart.

Alton did not instigate or lead in the activity. The desire, the aching need were mutual.

Paul's other arm wrapped around Alton's waist, with the hand firmly holding his buttock and keeping them pressed together; bulging crotch to bulging crotch. Two stiff dicks trapped in clothing pressed together between them.

As Paul's mouth moved over Alton's cheeks again, Alton surprised himself by letting out a little whimper of pleasure.

Finally, Paul spoke, just a whisper against his cheek, each syllable delivered in between kisses. "I've missed you. More than I ever thought possible." He took a breath. "I want you. So badly."

The words acted on Alton's body as much as anything physical could. His breathing became even heavier as he let out another moan, his head falling back allowing the taller man access to his neck for the delivery of more kisses. It had been months since Alton experienced passion like this, only ever with Paul.

Paul stepped back to pull off his top and then Alton's. Within an instant, he was back for another deep kiss. Their pelvises pushed together, feeling every inch of one another as their bodies rubbed together. Their hands explored each other's bare chests, arms, and toned, muscled, young skin. The excitement increased with the intimacy.

Alton had wondered if anything like this was possible with Paul, at West Beach. His question was answered.

"I've missed touching you." Paul's voice, a low, breathless whisper, sounded loud in this small pace. "I like touching you here."

Both hands ran over Alton's shoulders and down his arms, caressing his strong biceps and deltoids before returning to his chest. The tips of Paul's fingers brushed over the nipples on their way downwards.

Alton wanted to explode, in many ways, as Paul's hand pushed inside the elastic waistband of the sweatpants. In a cupboard, pushed close together, kissing the man of his dreams. And that man had a hold of his cock.

With his heart thundering in his chest, Alton didn't want this ever to end, but he doubted his ability to hold back. It had been way too long since he'd come with someone else. Since he'd come with Paul's hand on his dick in the special times they used to share. His legs went weak, and he almost lost consciousness, just for a moment.

Paul pushed him down onto the padded box-seat and dropped to his knees. With some difficulty, he tugged the pants down to Alton's ankles. Paul's mouth engulfed Alton's cock in a tight warm cavern of erotic pleasure. A pleasure that rippled through his body as Paul sucked him in slowly and then withdrew almost completely and repeated the movement.

Alton would have liked to enjoy these sensations over and over, but that wasn't going to happen this morning. He shut his eyes, tight and whimpered. "Oh yes."

Paul's hands were on his balls.

"I'm going to." Without leaving the seat, he thrust into Paul's mouth, which clamped firmly around his pulsing cock.

It released.

Alton didn't need to open his eyes; he could feel, Paul swallow as if he didn't need to breathe. Alton eventually opened his eyes in time to see Paul let the sated cock drop from his lips. His deep blue eyes looked into Alton's and a familiar expression of tightening muscles took over his dreamy-handsome face.

A deep, rumbling, primitive sound, unlike anything else, came from deep within and Alton leaned forwards, sure it was too late to help but he might be just in time to watch.

Paul's entire body arched, stiffly and, after some swift hand movements, he held his cock steady as white ribbons of cream shot into his hand and across the floor. A sight that stirred further feelings of unsatisfied lust within Alton.

Five months apart meant they had a lot of lost time to catch up on and to judge by his behavior, Paul felt that too. He slumped a little and Alton wanted to get down there with him, but there wasn't space.

Paul looked up with a twinkle in his eyes and a pleased-with-himself grin across his cheeks. He reached out for some tissues to clean himself up and wipe the evidence of their pleasure from the floor.

Alton grinned back. "I thought we were going to talk."

"We can talk, but I'm glad we did this." Still smiling, Paul looked like his limbs were made of rubber, he shook and stumbled as he tried to stand.

Alton held out a hand to help and pulled Paul toward him.

"Did I tell you I've missed you?" *And more, so much more.*

Paul flopped onto Alton's lap and commenced with more kisses as if he could never get enough. Speaking with his lips rubbing against Alton's. "This is the beat off room, but I think it's usually done on your own."

The taste of cock and seed on Paul, combined with the smell of sex in the room was thrilling, and Alton thought they'd be ready to continue soon. Yet, he couldn't fight back the anxiety that crept into the pit of his stomach as he faced reality. Another day of induction lay before him in this new world they lived in.

In their former home, they were secret lovers in an asexual world. Then they'd believed they were the only people with these primitive, natural urges. At WB they discovered many men and women, albeit an unusual minority, still had sexual desires.

Knowing Paul still wanted him wasn't enough to ease Alton's fears when both their lives in this new place depended on something he couldn't do—perform with women.

He wasn't ready to discuss his anxiety about the work at West Beach with Paul.

Wondering if this, what just happened, was merely a meaningless physical thing, Alton said, "You know I've got another tough day of training ahead of me." *I'm letting you off the hook.*

"Yeah? Yeah. I suppose you have. Sorry if this causes a problem." Paul reached for their tops and, holding one out for Alton, he stood up.

Alton bent over to sort out his pants. *Causes a problem! What the fuck?* Alton started to feel a little sick and a lot claustrophobic.

"I gotta go." Alton stood up, grabbed his top and pushed past quickly opening the door and exiting into the passage before Paul could say anything else. As he stepped into the cramped corridor, the cold air hit him, bringing him to his senses. Despite his own confusion and anxiety, he didn't want the door to close on Paul like this.

"Thanks, mate." Alton grabbed the door before it shut and looked into Paul's eyes. "That was one of the best things that's ever happened to me. And I've missed you so bad it hurts. Now, will you show me the way back?"

Appearing a little stunned, Paul visibly relaxed. He took a deep breath and smiled. With his sweater still in one hand, he stepped out into the corridor, which inevitably meant bringing them close together again. Skin to skin. He planted a quick, chaste kiss on Alton's lips and pushed past to lead the way along the narrow passage.

"Let's get dressed," Paul said over his shoulder as he pulled his top over his head. As if Alton may not have heard he repeated, "Let's get dressed first."

A small crowd of the unit's younger men including the other three who arrived the same day as Alton were sitting around outside, a short distance from the African drumming ensemble but far enough away to speak and be heard.

After several days at West Beach, Alton realized he was unlikely to run into Paul frequently by chance, not as a new boy on induction, at least. He certainly didn't expect to see him twice in one day, so he wasn't looking out for anything other than an opportunity to get away from everyone and hide in his bed, bringing to a close the worst day yet of his induction.

The day had started so well, meeting up with Paul. And what a meeting! At least one of the questions in Alton's mind had been answered. Paul still wanted the same physical contact, the way they touched each other in their former home.

They'd not talked. They could have done but Alton was scared. They had never discussed their feelings before, life was so simple at The Foresters so there had been no need for such a conversation. Now, Alton wasn't sure he could voice what he wanted to say. He wasn't sure he'd like Paul's reaction.

Anxiety about everything else at West Beach hung like a cloud.

The most embarrassing ST lesson yet took place in the afternoon. A joint session in which three boys were meant to fuck the lady in turn while the others watched and learned. The mentors stressed the newbies should lose their inhibitions if they were going to be good at the job, and apparently, lots of clients booked more than one man at a time.

For Alton, the experience had been the most excruciating experience so far and it was witnessed by teammates, Mo and Brandon. Brandon was about two or three years older, with that much more experience to share.

What torture, the peer pressure to perform. Failure was not an option.

It was certainly interesting to watch the other two men with Freya. Freya and Walsh were in control of his session, a blessing perhaps, since at least he was with women who understood his lack of progress to date.

Skillful and careful, Brandon was a contrast to Mo and his enthusiastic approach, which lacked the finesse of experience. With the memory of Paul fresh in Alton's mind, the smell of him still in his nose, and sex taking place right before his eyes, Alton was aroused. It was hot and exciting. He was aware of his pulse racing and his heavy breathing.

But there was no way that would translate into burying his erection inside his training partner for the first time. He didn't want it to happen; it just couldn't. Freya must have known that too. He shut his eyes and thought of men, not just Paul, but the men he'd just watched, as Freya sucked his cock for the first time.

Sitting outside with the other team, Mark's team of Cecil and Roy, as the day came to an end, random other young men all of whom could only be a few years into their West Beach careers came to join them. Introductions were made, jokes were made, and the men chattered about nothing.

It wasn't over, the ordeal of the day wasn't over. The boys were regrouping along with a couple of the mentors. The new recruits wanted to retell their experiences. Alton sunk into the chair quietly wishing the earth would swallow him as he had nothing to add to this conversation.

To make matters worse, Paul came over to join the crowd at precisely this moment, in perfect time to witness Alton's humiliation. Paul, who was obviously settling in well to West Beach work, was accompanied by a handsome man with white-blond hair and blue eyes. They seemed comfortable with each other as they stood together; their arms brushed against each other and they exchanged knowing smiles.

Alton recognized a pang of jealous anxiety when he couldn't help noting that the young blond stranger was similar to himself. He might be competing for Paul's attention with this pretty-faced youth.

"Look lads. We don't usually talk about what went on inside those rooms once the job's done," Roy interjected.

"We do," mumbled Mark. Damn right. Since arriving sex and women had dominated the conversation among the new boys.

Alton picked up his drink, a cloudy gas of lemonade, it gave him something to focus on other than the surrounding men.

"Yeah. You might enjoy it. But sometimes it's not so good and sometimes it's even embarrassing," said Brandon, he appeared ready to say more, but Roy interrupted.

"The bottom line is we all do that sort of work almost every day, sometimes with more than one client a day, various scenarios so talking about it back here later just gets boring."

A crowd of younger men gathered around. All apparently interested in talking about sex with women, despite what Roy claimed.

If Alton thought this might be a reprieve, he was to be disappointed.

"It's new to us, so not boring at all," said Mark. "Am I right lads?"

Nodding of heads and the chorus of, "Yeah," signaled general agreement.

"You never even got your turn today." As if to change the focus of debate, Mo spoke in a sincere way but landed him right in the spotlight.

Alton concentrated on not giving any reaction. He did not need to reply, although the others jumped in with comments.

"What do you mean?" asked Cecil.

"I mean Brandon had a go, I had a go, lovely girl but Alton here..." Mo didn't finish his thought.

"Ha!" Mark's face looked overjoyed at the opportunity to mock the man from his former home. "I wondered if you'd have it in you, Alton. This work takes a very special kind of man, and you might find yourself kicked outta here."

Mark, Cecil, Roy were laughing along with some of the other men who had gathered around. The three men who'd actually been in the session, Mo and Brandon and Alton, weren't smiling. Getting kicked out might have been a relief except that Paul was here, and he might be a reason to stay.

Alton showed no reaction.

"Nah, it wasn't like that," Mo raised his voice to be heard.

"No, it wasn't," agreed Brandon as the mocking laughter calmed down. "Our team was with the girl Alton has been training with all week, so I guess he knows her body pretty well."

Alton looked down, not wanting to make eye contact with anyone, especially Paul.

"Oh yeah?" Questioned Mark, who derived his sense of importance from stamping on others. "Have you touched her, Alton? Have you fucked her or chickened out?"

The crowd went silent. Maybe the crowd wanted to hear what Alton had to say.

"He doesn't have to tell us, it's private," said Roy.

"I don't think Alton's a virgin after what we saw today, do you Mo?" said Brandon,

"I'd say he's got a good thing going with his training partner. He's doing stuff I'll bet the rest of you haven't tried yet."

Alton couldn't prevent a small smile creeping onto his face, as those comments would certainly take the wind out of the sails of that annoying jerk, Mark. He liked the way Brandon had made him sound mysterious, even in front of Paul. Paul knew him so very well in that way. Alton just hoped Mo wouldn't reveal all; a bit of mystery was a good thing.

Alton looked around and saw everyone focused on Brandon and Mo waiting for more details, but Mo just nodded and Brandon had clearly finished.

"I stand corrected then," Mark said, "Sorry mate. You're so quiet, who'd think you've got something special with the ladies?"

Alton came out of the conversation looking pretty good, saved by the good grace of his training partner Freya, in his opinion.

Mark also impressed his new friends. Apologizing, admitting you when you're wrong—people liked that in a man. And that was the final impression. The fact that Mark had been happy to bully and humiliate Alton if at all possible was forgotten all too soon by most people.

"What was the girl like for your session?" Mo asked Cecil, moving the conversation forward.

A firm hand gripped Alton's shoulder; a familiar voice whispered in his ear. "Let's go for a walk."

CHAPTER SEVEN
Paul

After the amazing way they came together and the weird way they parted that morning, Paul was relieved he'd canceled his client. The last thing he wanted to do was get hands on with someone else, after spending such a wonderful, intimate time with Alton.

Instead of hitting the track or joining in some team sports, as he usually would after getting his chores out of the way, Paul hung out for the afternoon with his roommate, Jay.

Always fun company, Jay was an enigma and the community clown. Frivolous until he sat in front of a piano or got with a client. Paul knew how Jay behaved with clients because they'd shared a few.

Paul, who hadn't learned any musical instrument, sat in on Jay's piano practice in the afternoon.

Following the beautifully flowing classical music, Jay hammered away at a style he was learning, "ragtime" he called it. Paul listened quietly and day-dreamed of Alton. He'd love the music and Paul wondered if he'd like Jay.

Of course, he would, everyone likes Jay.

The way the day started so well put Paul in such a good mood. He would have liked more time with Alton, but perhaps they'd meet up tomorrow and every morning. And when the induction was completed, they could spend more time together.

The day turned to evening and Paul was still floating on a high when he walked towards the recreation hub with Jay. Zander performing on drums always promised a great atmosphere, but Jay would miss most of it. He had to leave early to make an appointment with an evening client.

As they approached the direction of the drumming, Jay and Paul were drawn toward a buzzing crowd of younger men who had settled a little distance away from the music. The group was talking, laughing and comparing notes on their training sessions. Paul spotted Alton. Their eyes met briefly, and he noticed Alton checking Jay out, too, before looking away.

It became obvious that a group training event had taken place. Paul remembered them from his first few weeks of induction. An experienced couple had sex and then the new trainees replicated the action in front of a small audience of their fellow students. He smiled as he remembered these fun sessions; Paul enjoyed showing off in front of the other guys. Hearing the conversation unfold, he imagined that Alton, as his complete opposite, hated every moment.

Before he reached Alton, to ask him to come away to talk, Mark started poking fun at him. Paul froze. Rage surged through his veins, and he had a chivalrous urge to protect the younger man. Paul didn't ever want to see Alton treated like that.

Brandon spoke up, defending Alton and maintaining some mystery around what had happened. In that moment, Paul decided he liked Brandon and elevated him to a new high as a nice guy and potential ally. Did Paul need allies? He might.

Taking a deep breath with absolutely no idea what might happen, he approached Alton.

"What was the girl like for your session?"

He heard the guys continuing their conversation. As he placed his hand on Alton's shoulder and bent down to whisper in his ear. "Let's walk."

"Hi, Paul." Mark jumped up, enthusiastically greeting his old friend. "What a great place we got here."

"Yeah, haven't we?" Paul replied coldly. He didn't return the smile and had no inclination to stay and chat but couldn't just walk away with Alton, not now that all eyes were fixed on him.

"Lads, this is Paul, back from my hometown. Paul, meet Cecil and Mo. They arrived here at the same time as us. Of course, you know Alton."

Heads nodded, hands were held up in a greeting and the murmur of "Hi," went around.

"I guess you might know the others as they've all been here longer than us?" Mark wasn't giving up, always a talker who loved to be at the center of things.

"Yeah," Paul said again. "Look, I got to talk with Alton so let's catch up later."

Alton sat still and dignified as he had through the humiliating banter a few minutes earlier, and Paul placed a hand on his shoulder.

"Sure. Some things never change. You two always were best buddies, always disappearing together." Mark waved a hand as if to dismiss them.

They didn't need Mark's permission to leave.

"Anyway, don't hide away for too long; it would be good to catch up."

Paul seethed inside. As if he would have any desire to talk to odious Mark or any man who derived satisfaction from humiliating Alton.

The group of men returned to talking among themselves, with no one but Mark giving any attention to the departing couple. Alton stood, and the couple walked away in silence toward the open grounds that were disappearing in the low light of the evening gloom.

"Let's just keep walking," Paul said, glancing at Alton.

"Just like old times, some things don't change. You and me, walking away from the group." Alton sounded happy even though the words were open to many interpretations.

Paul glanced again to see a big smile on his friend's face. Paul grinned as well, feeling like he'd won a super prize. "And since when did you get so happy?"

"I've been saving it up for almost six months. If you saw me at Foresters without you, then you'd understand. And I deserve a big dose of happiness after surviving the trip here on a boat with Mark as the only male for company."

"I don't want to speak or even think about that self-centered, selfish, arrogant..." Paul clenched his fists. Mark had never bothered him, but he hated the thought of anyone trying to belittle Alton.

"That's easy for you to say. I've been on induction with him all week. I've had about as much as I can stand just traveling here. Speaking of which, where are we going?"

"I don't know where," said Paul.

"That'd be like this morning then. And look how that turned out."

"It turned out quite well; didn't it?" Paul couldn't stop his face breaking into a grin, and he felt his cheeks flush with color. "You might have noticed, there is almost nowhere to go to get away from everyone here. Not like at The Foresters." He glanced at Alton as they walked.

"It's not like The Foresters; that's true. So where have you been? I managed not to see you for days."

Paul heard the hurt in the question. *You have no idea how difficult it can be here.*

"Have you been around the village?" Without waiting for an answer Paul added, "This is the village."

They'd walked only a short distance from the main building, which dominated the view on the horizon from any direction. The collection of densely packed small buildings were visible from the recreation area and only a five-minute walk away. Hundreds of wooden chalets were laid out in a grid formation and commonly referred to as the village.

"I'm in E12, with Zander, who you met this morning. I don't know if you saw him playing one of the drums tonight."

"No. I didn't notice. I saw the guy with you tonight, though."

"Jay? He's in our room too. He couldn't stay and hang out with us because he had a booking. Come on, I'll show you my room."

The huts were arranged so that there was enough space for men to pass between them on narrow paths, but they were close enough together that if Paul spread his arms wide apart he'd be able to touch one with each hand.

"These huts are all new, just put here a few months ago."

"Really?"

"Well, some have been here a long time but most are new. We were very cramped in the main building before. I guess there might be empty rooms there now, but at least we have more space."

Paul stopped, they had arrived at E12.

Their eyes met, something intense and unspoken passed between them igniting something deep inside Paul. He led the way up the steps, opened the door, entered, and flicked on a light.

Alton stared at the switch as if it were an extraordinary treasure. At The Foresters, old farm buildings, pre-dating Matriarchy, were full of switches that did nothing. The electricity from solar panels and wind turbines was limited and rationed in the primitive habitat.

"Instant light when you want it. It's something you get used to quickly." Could Alton be talking about something else? Like getting used to their separation or this new world?

"It gets easier, it really does." Paul hoped he was saying the right thing, but he was uncertain. "I share this room with three others. Two of them are with clients now, and we can hear Zander from here."

Alton stayed by the door, as if he didn't intend to stay or was waiting for an invitation. He looked about the room. Three sets of bunk beds, space for six men. A table in the middle of the room with six chairs. Cupboards, sink. Electric light. Basic but more spacious and luxurious than any bedroom Paul had ever seen before coming here and he guessed Alton might be thinking the same.

"I've not seen inside any of these buildings," Alton said, finally walking into the middle of the room, closer to Paul.

"The best ones are a few blocks back; they have fewer occupants and more luxuries."

Though E12 was luxurious. Paul knew Alton couldn't see or imagine the hidden heating system that should keep it warm in winter. Nor could he see that instant warm water also poured into the basin at the movement of a lever.

"That's where the big earners live. Just one or two guys to a cabin. You've seen the leaderboard?"

Alton nodded and stepped up to Paul so that their faces were just inches apart. "I see you as a big earner. How can anyone resist you?"

Paul leaned forward and kissed Alton on the lips, an almost innocent quick peck, nothing like the kisses they had previously shared. "I'm only interested in you finding me irresistible."

"I do." Alton put his hands on Paul's waist.

Paul copied, enveloping Alton in his embrace. "Look. Just because we're both here at WB, it doesn't mean we'll get much chance to see each other, not in these first few weeks of your induction. They keep you busy. We're all kept busy but especially you new recruits. You'll go to bed exhausted."

"That's true so far."

"It will change in a few weeks. They will integrate you in with the rest of us. We'll see more of each other then."

"Great." Alton's flat tone of voice suggested he wasn't thinking great things at all but his wide eyes looked directly into Paul's and their faces remained just an inch apart.

The room buzzed with sexual chemistry. Despite the morning's amorous assignation, Paul only hoped to hang out with his friend on their next encounter and show him around. But alone and face-to-face, the desire to touch him was stronger than ever. Paul didn't expect this, didn't plan it.

Paul broke eye contact and moved to draw the curtains. Lined, thick material hung at the four small windows. Windows positioned in such a way that it was unlikely people would look in the hut, but he didn't want to take the chance.

Alton walked toward the door. Had Paul misread the signals? *Please don't walk out.*

"Shame there's no lock." Alton grabbed a nearby chair and wedged it under the handle. He turned and pulled off his top. What he lacked in height, he made up for in breadth; shorter than Paul but broader, stronger and heavier. His muscular physique was obvious even when covered by clothes. Thick arms and broad shoulders. A muscled and perfectly sculpted torso with pecs and abs more developed than ever they were back when Paul lived at the Foresters.

Paul had touched that body this morning but now was able to stand back and admire it.

Paul took a deep breath.

Fucking sexy.

He'd always enjoyed looking at Alton, and touching him.

As if reading Paul's mind and aware of the effect he had on Paul, Alton smiled seductively. "Which is your bed?"

"Bottom," Paul replied, pointing as if he lost the use of his words in full sentences as well as the movement in his legs.

Alton walked to the bed, kicked off his shoes, dropped his sweater on top of them and lay back. With his hands on top of his head, he casually flaunted a fit body and flexed biceps.

"When are your dorm-mates likely to come back?"

"It could be anytime, an hour, two or more." Paul was rooted to the spot, enjoying the view, drooling at the overtly sexual come on.

Alton was well aware of what turned Paul on, as was apparent by the way he was presenting it to him in his bed. Paul had always enjoyed seeing Alton's bare chest and muscles when they were at The Foresters. The way he ran his fingers and kisses over Alton's body must have made it clear even though he'd said nothing.

They'd never spoken about it, about what they did together or how it made them feel. They just did what they did.

Paul couldn't remember such sexual tension between them before, such a sense of excited anticipation existed inside E12.

In their old home, they were friends who fucked. They didn't talk about it. They didn't need to; they'd grown up together and seen each other every day. Absence over the past five months had changed things. West Beach had changed things.

Paul loved looking at and touching Alton's body but couldn't remember Alton presenting himself like this before, and he liked it, a lot.

"Are you going to join me?"

He was getting hot and wanted to get naked, but Paul followed Alton's lead and just removed his top, dropping it on the wooden floor.

Heart pounding in his chest, he took off his boots and straddled the man lying wantonly atop his sheets. Legs either side, crotch to crotch, Paul lowered his open mouth to claim the kiss he desired. Sloppy and passionate. Savoring the sensation of Alton's bare chest against his own.

"I thought we'd talk," Paul mumbled when they broke apart for air.

"We should." Alton's mouth would not leave the surface of Paul's skin for more than a few seconds, and he continued to kiss Paul's chin, neck, whatever he could reach. "Let's talk later."

Propped on one arm, Paul moved his free hand over the smooth skin mapping the firm muscles beneath. His tongue was in Alton's mouth, but Paul wanted to drag it across Alton's body. Taste him. Explore every bulge of his developed muscles, the curve of his pectorals dipping into the valleys of definition. From his right arm, across his shoulders, over his chest, and down the left arm.

Paul was on top of the most attractive person alive, and he would never get enough of him.

Propped up on one elbow he used his free hand to explore the sexy body on his bed as they continued to kiss. He worked his way down between them and slipped one hand inside Alton's pants to find his hard dick.

A gasp escaped Alton's mouth.

Paul hoped Zander, Rayfe, and Jay would not be back for ages. Sex in his room seemed way riskier than he was comfortable with. It wasn't what he'd imagined doing when they'd entered, and with no lock on the door anyone could drop in.

The chair propped against the door did little to assure Paul of their privacy. He didn't want to stop either; both men were way beyond that. Up until that morning, they'd gone a long time without touching each other.

"I've got to..." Somewhat abruptly Paul climbed off the bed and made it clear what he had to do.

Paul swiftly pulled off his jeans and underwear, Alton shuffled and shimmied his pants with undergarments down to his knees. Paul grabbed them and pulled them off completely. Without a word Paul got back on top of Alton, taking both of their cocks in one hand and rubbing them together with a greater urgency than before.

"Wait." Alton pushed and shuffled so that the two of them lay facing each other on the small bed, their legs entwined. Face to face, mouth to mouth, chest to chest, sharing a need to be close to each other in every way. They lay next to each other and, with their hands, brought each other to climax.

Tension relieved, for a short while, Paul grabbed a towel to clean them both up. Alton pulled on his trousers and slipped under the blankets.

"I didn't expect any of this when I showed you in here."

"And the problem with it is?" Alton looked content and sleepy.

"No problem but I guess I got my answer." Paul pulled on his trousers, aware their solitude might be disturbed at any moment. Paul looked down at his lover.

"You got an answer? And the question is what?" Alton asked.

"Do you want us to carry on as we used to at The Foresters?" Paul slipped in between the sheets for a cuddle. "It can't be the same. This place is so different that nothing will be the same."

Paul thought he saw Alton's face tense though his eyes were shut, and he didn't speak for minutes. Paul wondered whether he'd done something wrong.

"So what do we do?" Alton asked.

"I've been trying to figure it out since I got here."

"What's your answer to the same question? Do you want things to carry on the same as before?" Alton said after a silence of minutes.

"I want things to be the same."

As soon as he said it Paul wondered why he had. It wasn't true. He didn't want things to be the same, he wanted something better. He wanted something special with Alton but not a step back to how things were. Before he could explain, he tensed. He heard voices. The music? They could still hear music, but it wasn't the same drumming sound.

Paul shot out of bed, and Alton followed. The bedclothes were a rumpled mess, and there was no time to get the rest of their clothing back on.

"Sit down," whispered Paul, touching Alton's chest almost to push him down and a spark of arousal from the touch teased him despite the urgency of the situation.

With Alton sitting on his bed instead of lying in it, Paul decided to move the barricade from the door to avoid difficult questions. Just in time. He was standing right by the door when three men burst through and crashed straight into him.

CHAPTER EIGHT
Paul

"Whoa. You made me jump," said Jay, he was the first through the door.

Zander and Rayfe followed, and all three stared at the stranger in the room, sitting on Paul's messed up bed.

"Hi," said Alton.

Alton remained seated as per Paul's instructions, which he hoped would help to hide the unmade bed.

"Lads, this is Alton, my little brother from home, but as you can see, he's not so little anymore." Paul's introduction flowed with fast-thinking logic. "He's bulked up in just the six months that I've been here. We were just comparing..." Talking too much to cover up the truth in his mind, Paul was spared by interruptions from his roommates who weren't listening. They were keen to speak to Alton.

"Little brother, welcome to our cave." Zander, the tallest and oldest of the three, pulled up a chair close to the bed where Alton was sitting. "Didn't we meet this morning?"

"Yes." Alton nodded.

"This is Jay, and that sleepy head is Rayfe." Zander pointed out the two other men.

Rayfe waved from a bottom bunk bed across the room where he flopped. "Excuse me. My mind is still awake, but my body is not."

"Rayfe, don't be rude, we have a guest!" Jay pulled up a chair very close to Alton. "I don't know if Paul's given you the run-down of E12?"

Barely pausing for breath Jay chattered on.

"Allow me. Zee's the grandad in the room, grown up and sensible. Ray's Mr. Romantic. He charms all the women with magical words and falls in love with them himself. Paul is the baby and the heartthrob of the room, obviously. Of course, you already know Paul." Jay was all smiles, delighted to have someone new to talk to.

"I can't help the effect I have on people." Paul sorted out their clothes and handed Alton his top.

"Call me romantic but I can't help falling in love." Rayfe called out. "I am pleased to meet you, by the way, particularly from the horizontal position of my bed. Please forgive me for that."

"It's okay. I really like being horizontal too." Alton and Paul were pulling on their T-shirts.

"So what's with the topless look?" Zander asked.

Alton had picked up on Paul's excuse that no-one listened to when they first entered the room. "I was showing Paul how I'd bulked up in the months since he left Foresters. I did most, not all, of the heavy lifting there. We were comparing definition."

"Have you met Rod yet? He's always pumping iron in the gym," said Jay. "I don't think he's got a room to go to—just lives permanently cuddled up to those weights in the gym."

"Yes. I've met him. I've only been here a week, and he's tried to chase me outta there. Scared I'll get bigger than him."

"What kind of weights were you doing back home to build up a body like that?" Zander asked.

"Sacks of potatoes mostly."

The men laughed. They all remembered the hardships of their childhoods in the far-flung, rural men's units.

The lads chatted about the gym, exercise and sport for a while along with tales of their former homes. Paul's roommates accepted the excuse for undress without question as no one usually arrived with upper body development like Alton's. There wasn't the same leisure time and facilities at other men's units, outside of West Beach.

"What do you think is the best thing about WB, compared to your old home?" asked Rafe from his bed. "The gym?"

Alton glanced at Paul. "The company."

"Not the women?" Jay looked a little surprised.

"I know what he means. The thought that I might have turned into one of those elders haunts me as I get older." Zander shook his head and shuddered, now in his mid-thirties.

"You'd be an elder-elder by now." Jay could never resist reminding the older man just how old he was.

"And doesn't that show how different we are here. The elders were old but they might not even be thirty years old. Here men under forty are still young, and even the old men are in demand for their virile performance with the customers." Rayfe lay on his side on his bottom bunk, he appeared comfortable but still part of the conversation.

"You mean even our old men don't sit around and nap for most of the day?" Jay said.

"Another difference I find strange is the medication. We all had it at The Foresters, every day. Here no one has it." Alton couldn't explain why this preyed on his mind when nobody else seemed to wonder about it. He suspected the other new guys were so overwhelmed discovering sex with the opposite sex for the first time that they didn't question anything else. But Alton discovered pleasures of the flesh with Paul years earlier and wasn't terribly interested in the new fare on offer.

"Medication?" Rayfe looked confused or was it sleepy? "Oh, yes. I'd forgotten. I haven't thought about it in years."

"I remember the medicine for the virus," said Jay. He always had something to say, and Paul found it rather endearing. "You know we didn't all get the same stuff; they just told us we did."

"What do you mean?" Alton asked.

The others waited, knowing Jay couldn't finish there, without an elaborate explanation.

"A couple of us wondered if there might be a link between the medicine and who gets to leave. It stands to reason if all the men at the farm were sick from the virus then why would any of them leave and why even bother with the medication? We thought perhaps some guys got cured and then left, so we started monitoring it."

"The security was lax to none-existent, we could go in and sniff around any time. We started cleaning the sick bay, so we'd have a legit reason if we got caught rummaging about. We worked out that all the adults were on one kind of medicine whereas some boys were on a totally different type. We weren't able to monitor long enough before I was transferred here but I'm pretty sure it was us boys who left that were given a different medication and from a young age."

"That matches what someone else has told me." Alton looked serious and fascinated by Jay's story.

"Paul, you can ask your favorite client about this," Zander said.

"Who?" He felt uncomfortable talking about clients with Alton present though he wasn't sure why. It was just a job and one that he had no choice but to do.

"Kerry. She's some scientist and works with the government so she might know about it." Zander looked at Alton to explain as if everyone else in the room would already know. "She's totally smitten with Paul."

Paul wanted to hide, to get Alton out of there, and to shut Zander up: all of those in any order. "It's certainly not a mutual feeling." He spat the words out just a little too forcefully.

As if he hadn't heard the last comment Rayfe said, "If I remember I'll ask Mia about it. She's a fertility scientist; she might know something." He had a dreamy look on his face as he spoke.

Jay rolled his eyes. "You might not be in love, Paul, but he is." He nodded his head in Rayfe's direction.

In love!

"Alton, Rayfe has been moping about for months like he was sickening for something. It was kind of a relief just to find out he had a favorite client," Jay explained.

Alton instantly fitted in with the E12 dream team. Surrounded by his favorite people, Paul was pleased his secret lover got along so well with this crowd.

Paul also hoped to have lots more opportunities to see Alton with his top off but knew his feelings weren't driven only by pure lust. Lust and desire, definitely, but lust and desire drove the clients who booked appointments. Between them there was something more.

In love.

Those two words resonated with Paul.

CHAPTER NINE
Alton

After the best night's sleep in a long time, Alton woke up feeling well rested and more content than he had in months. Reunited with Paul, making a physical connection, and getting on well with his roommates helped, as did breaking the stretch of involuntary celibacy and emotional isolation.

They didn't get to speak in private about the things on his mind but, frankly; he became so distracted when alone with Paul. They had more pressing matters on their minds.

Alton hadn't voiced the things he burned to say, but they communicated without words.

The way Paul touched him told him so much more than Paul had ever said aloud. It also satisfied a more urgent basic physical need. While Alton didn't have all the answers, he thought they were both a bit clearer about what they wanted from each other even though they hadn't discussed it. They wanted each other.

They'd never discussed it.

Paul was definitely into him in a big way judging by the eagerness of his actions. The ingredients were there for a better future for the two of them together, if it weren't for the work, if it weren't for West Beach.

Another day of education and training. Things went downhill as each day passed.

Freya and Walsh put Alton under no pressure to perform. They were full of reassurances. Nevertheless, the implication was there; they expected Alton to fuck women, if not soon, then eventually. At least the sessions didn't usually involve other men and Alton's mentor, Max, didn't witness his humiliation. If you could call it humiliating when Alton didn't even try.

He just couldn't find it in himself, not an ounce of attraction to women.

Alton couldn't imagine it would ever happen. He lived each day with rising anxiety about what that would mean for his future at WB but tried not to dwell on it.

In the evening Paul showed up by the pool with his roommates Zander, Jay, and Rayfe. Their eyes met, but Paul did not single him out for conversation. That might appear too conspicuous. They didn't want to draw attention to themselves.

Alton had an idea. He left the group and then waited out of sight to see if Paul would follow him. After a lengthy time, when he was about to give up and go alone to the library or the gym or just to bed, Paul followed.

"There you are. I wondered where you were off to," Paul said.

"Hello, handsome. I hoped you'd come and find me."

"Why's that?"

"There's something I need to practice, and I hoped you'd come along because I can't do it on my own." Without explaining, Alton set off, leading the way to the gym.

There were men in the gym; there were always men in the gym, working out, on the mats, lifting weights, stretching. The loud music drowned out conversation.

"I want to perfect my massage techniques," Alton announced in a loud voice so that not just Paul but anyone who might be nearby and paying attention would hear. "Cray said we can use the massage rooms any time."

Alton led the way to the furthest small room, they stepped inside and closed the door. The music sounded muffled from within the room.

"This seems pretty private to me," said Alton. "We won't be interrupted in here."

"Good thinking, I don't know why I never thought of this except that I don't come to the gym much."

"We never got to talk much last night. I think we can talk here."

"Yeah, you're right. No one will hear us here with that loud music outside. We can talk but you do know we can't do more." Paul looked toward the clear pane of glass, the window in the door. It looked into a small vestibule where other doors led into other massage rooms or cupboards.

Alton placed the room-in-use sign on the door. "Yeah, of course, no lock. I don't know what you got on your mind, but I was just going to give you a massage."

"Sure, just that," Paul replied. Tall and slim, Paul's short black hair stood up in all directions in a unique, just-got-out-of-bed style. "And talk too."

"So, get your clothes off and lie down, face down. If anyone looks in we won't appear as if we are doing something we're not supposed to."

"Okay," Paul agreed, stripping off his top without hesitation.

As he undressed, Paul's deep blue eyes, like the sea under the summer sky, didn't break eye contact. Instead, they challenged Alton to watch or look away.

"Everything off?" Paul asked as he dropped his pants on the floor.

"Yes. Easiest that way." Alton could not help licking his lips as he watched. He had no intention of looking away.

Seeing Paul in person again just confirmed that Alton's memories of a gorgeous body were not just in his fantasy. Paul looked stunning, tempting, and Alton wondered how he would control his desire as he touched this man.

He didn't just get on the bed. Once naked, Paul stood by the massage couch and stretched. He raised his arms, pushed out his chest, and rolled his shoulders back. A smattering of black hair had only recently appeared on his chest, trailing down across his flat stomach, a line leading to dark, wiry pubes and a semi-erect dick.

He gave a smoldering look, pouting his lips. Kissable and teasing. His non-verbal language echoed loudly around the small room.

Look at me, do you want me?

Alton took a gulp and turned away to find the massage oil. He'd seen Paul without clothes many times, along with all the other men. They lived together, and things like communal showers were normal. Nudity didn't embarrass him. But Paul was adorable and sexy but Alton wanted to stay calm and in control. He wanted to suck Paul's dick too.

"So, you want me to face down?" Paul asked.

"On your stomach might be best. Best if I have the same effect on you as you're having on me, and someone looks through that window." Alton chuckled.

Paul lay down on the massage couch, and Alton covered his lower half, from his feet to his ass, with a towel.

With his back to the door, Alton couldn't help bending down so that his face was only inches above his lover. He inhaled deeply. He resisted the temptation to bring his face so close that he could kiss and lick; that wouldn't constitute a massage.

Alton poured the blended massage oil directly onto the skin and pushed the liquid over the body. A subtle zesty citrus scent rose from the warm body. He ran his hands along either side of the spine. Up to the neck, across the shoulders and around down the sides to squeeze the obliques.

"It was nice..., I enjoyed yesterday," Alton said, it sounded so feeble, these words did not convey what he wanted to say at all.

"Mmm," replied Paul. "This feels good."

"It felt good being together last night. We aren't at Foresters anymore, but we could transfer to somewhere else together." The implication clear, he hoped. Somewhere where together, another men's unit, where they didn't have to have sex with women.

"We could just see how it goes here." Paul's body relaxed under the gentle touch and his sentences emerged slowly. "We're both new here after all."

It wasn't what Alton wanted to hear as his hands glided over his lover's smooth skin. "I don't see myself fitting in here."

"I know what you mean. I felt terrible by the end of my first week too. It does get better."

Alton remained quiet. He couldn't see how he'd ever fit in, but this thought left his mind due to the immediate distraction of Paul's naked skin and taut muscles under his hands.

Glancing at the door from the corner of his eye as he moved around the massage couch, a plan started to formulate in his mind. Enjoying the innocent massage, there was no pressure to do anything else.

"Do you want to know something?" asked Paul.

"What?" Alton's mind was still on their conversation about leaving this particular men's unit.

"What I'm thinking?"

"What are you thinking?" There must be somewhere else they could go. Alton couldn't envisage himself staying there and he didn't want to leave without Paul. Perhaps Paul had a solution.

Paul turned his head to face Alton. "I'm thinking of you. You underneath me. Of me burying my cock inside you, like I used to. I'm thinking about how incredible that was and feeling you come. I loved watching you as I fucked you and listening to the sounds you made."

It wasn't what he expected to hear, Alton was stunned, flattered and turned on all at once. He forgot his concerns as blood rushed to one part of his anatomy.

Paul bent his arm at his elbow and raised his head to support it on his hand. "I want to do that again. I wish it were happening right now. It was the best thing ever and I miss it."

Alton was thrilled to hear these words from Paul. "Really? You never said anything at the time."

"There was no reason to. I thought that we were the only people to do such stuff and that it would never end. Why would we talk about it?"

Alton had thought the same thing. They'd never talked so much about their feelings and desires for each other. Never needed to.

Paul didn't seem to expect an answer to his question. He continued, "Now. You must know how much I want you. The pressure is filling my whole body. It's in my stomach, my chest, my mouth. I feel like I might burst if I don't get more of you. There is no way we can just part after this, like friends, and then just expect to go to bed alone."

Alton moved the towel so that it covered Paul's lower back and just barely covered his ass.

Eyes bulging and head whirring, turned on and with a plan fully formulated Alton whispered in Paul's ear. "I'm not finished with you."

The greasy palms slipped under the towel to caress everywhere including the most private places. Sliding over Paul's fleshy cheeks, Alton skirted a finger along the crack of his ass and cupped his balls.

"I can imagine you on your back. I'd continue this massage. I'd run oil across your chest and stomach and bite your nipples and kiss my way down to your cock."

Paul groaned, and Alton noticed the movement of his hips as he ground into the firm mattress.

"Then I'd want to lie on that table and have you fuck me like you used to. I'd start on my back so I could watch you fuck me, face to face, you on top. After, I'd get on my knees. You'd make me come with your cock in me, and you'd come too, filling me. That's what I want." Saying the words aloud, partly just for fun, turned Alton on more. He pictured the scene and, yes, he craved it.

But they couldn't act on impulse, not here, not like they used to.

Alton shared his plan. "I know we can't do that now. Instead, we are going to move so we're out of sight of the door. If we're along the wall towards the corner, no one will see us if they look in the window and, of course, the light is on, the room in use sign is there, so anyone looking will assume someone is in here getting dressed."

"Okay. Let's do it." Paul needed no persuasion.

Paul got up off the table, his hard cock standing out at a right angle, and took the two strides to the corner. The room was tiny.

Alton, who was still fully dressed, fiddled with his own trousers to free his cock as he got on his knees in front of Paul. At first, he licked gently around the head and along the shaft, tip to root and back again.

Wrapping his fingers around Paul's hard dick and slipping his lips around the end, Alton slowly sucked it into his mouth. Inch by inch, slowly teasing as it went deeper and deeper. He let go of his own cock so he could use two hands on Paul.

He cupped, squeezed and gently pulled on his balls with his palm and extended his fingers to touch the soft area behind. All the time, continuing the motion on Paul's rigid shaft; sucking, licking and tugging. Alton's fingers slid behind, moving the length of the crack, teasing at the rear entrance, then grasping at Paul's ass cheeks.

Paul groaned, throwing his head back and thrusting his hips forwards.

Alton knew how turned on he was. To even say stuff like what he'd just said about the sexy stuff they used to do. The things they'd done but never talked about before. Paul obviously wanted Alton in this way too. This need for each other was entirely mutual.

He was aware of Paul's hand on his head, fingers pulling at his hair. He knew the signs. Paul's cock seemed to bounce and throb in his mouth. Paul pulled out a little, but Alton wasn't about to let him go.

He relaxed his throat, let his head fall head back wanting to taste Paul and feel him come on his tongue. With the explosion of delicious spunk in his mouth, Alton couldn't hold back his excitement. He pumped his dick in his hand and came too.

"Oh. Huh." An indeterminate grunt from a startled male voice.

Alton looked up only in time to see the door click shut behind the intruder. With a cock in each hand, and his left hand covered in his own seed, he dropped Paul's in order to wipe some stray Paul-cream from his chin.

"Did you see him? Who it was?" He looked up at Paul who was still looking at the door as if it held answers.

"No. He was gone so quickly."

CHAPTER TEN
Paul

The perfect way to spoil the end of a perfect day.

Caught having sex with someone you shouldn't. Caught having sex with someone you love and seeing the anguish on that man's face. Wanting to reassure him but not sure how.

After years of practice, Alton understood exactly how to please Paul. But the way Paul felt about Alton took any physical contact with the man into a different realm of gratification.

Remembering the image of Alton on his knees and fingers running through the mess of blond hair; he always looked like he just got out of bed. Alton looked fucking gorgeous. Even better now, six months older and fitter.

Funny in a strong silent type sort of way. He didn't say much, but what he said was worth listening to. The way he'd led him to that room. The way he'd touched him. The way he'd suggested that corner for something sexy. Everything about Alton was erotic and amazing.

Paul couldn't say how he felt; they'd never talked much about feelings. Standing there naked in that room with Alton on his knees at his feet; he could show him. He found him irresistible. It wasn't so much Alton giving him a blow job as

Paul thrusting like he needed it. He was entirely lost in ecstasy when the door opened.

The stranger.

The voice.

It happened too quickly for Paul or Alton to see who opened the door. They looked up, and the man had gone. Too fast for a response. They couldn't exactly chase the man through the gym because they were both compromised. Their bodies still recovering from the throes of orgasm. Paul was naked and Alton's legs were bound by half discarded clothing.

"Did you see his face?" Alton asked, anxiety in his face as he stood up, wiping himself on a towel.

"No, but the voice sounded familiar, I can't be sure, though." Paul pulled up his pants.

"I'm sorry, I know it's my fault, we shouldn't have." Alton looked so despondent.

No one should look so unhappy just moments after sharing something so intimate and erotic. Alton's distressed appearance upset Paul far more than the annoyance of being interrupted, he wanted to look after Alton, make him feel good. Not like this.

Paul reached out, hooked his thumbs through Alton's belt loops and pulled him close. Gazing into his tear-filled gray eyes near broke Paul's heart. "Don't say that. I'm not sorry we did it. I don't want to have to live without touching you. Whatever happens from now on, it is worth it."

Worth it because a blow job from a client he didn't care for bore no comparison to anything like what he experienced with Alton.

Paul moved his head forward to claim a kiss. His lips brushed lightly over Alton's slightly open mouth. Paul licked his lips and met no resistance breaking into Alton's mouth. Passionately and full of emotion they kissed. A kiss that said more than their limited words could convey.

"What do you think will happen?" Alton tried to pull away. He looked fearful and Paul held him tightly.

"Nothing. I've no idea. We didn't see him; perhaps he didn't see who we are."

"Perhaps we should go now?" Alton anxiously bit his bottom lip.

"No." Paul was emphatic. "We don't know when we might get more time together. Let's stay here a while. Come on, let's sit down here where we're out of view."

"Unless someone comes in the door," Alton mumbled miserably.

"We can hold hands and just be together." Paul slipped to the floor pulling Alton into his arms.

"Yes. I can do that. Give me the rundown on your roommates I met last night."

Paul talked about his roommates. Zander the drummer and someone who commanded a great deal of respect at the unit. The romantic Rayfe, a guitarist who had fallen in love with one of the clients. Paul wasn't sure how that would work. Men and women didn't generally form close emotional bonds.

Only a few years older than Alton and Paul, there was Jay. The most outgoing, fun personality in E12. Popular among all the men at West Beach. What could Paul say about Jay? He played the piano and talked a lot, too much, non-stop.

Paul didn't say anything about kissing Jay. About touching Jay only days before. It didn't mean anything, and it was just the briefest of caresses. It happened because a client asked them to kiss. Heterosexual and highly professional, Jay was willing to act upon a client's request and meet her fantasies. An action that touched on the edges of Paul's own fantasies. He hadn't told anyone that he liked guys in that way.

Paul didn't want to talk to Alton about the work with clients whether it involved another man or not.

It was about an hour later that Alton and Paul got off the floor, tidied up the room, and left. It was uneventful, in that no one else burst in on them and when they left, the gym was empty. It was late, dark and most men would be in bed. They went their separate ways, Alton returning to his room upstairs in the old main building.

Paul had barely stepped outside the main building on route to his cabin in the village when he heard his name.

A loud whisper formed a name. "Paul."

Paul turned to see Mark loitering in the dark. He faced the door Paul had just come through. Had he been waiting for him?

"What's up, Mark? Are you okay?" Paul moved closer but did not sit.

"No." Mark shook his head slowly. He sat down on a bench, his shoulders slumped.

"I've been walking around for this past hour trying to get that scene out of my head. You know, the thing you wish you'd never seen, but it leaves a permanent image on the inside of your eyelids." Mark seemed upset; his head hung low, and he stared at the floor, not looking Paul in the eye.

"What are you telling me?" asked Paul, taking a couple of steps closer.

"I went into the gym, and I saw him giving you a massage. Thought nothing of it, we were told to practice. I left you for a while and then when I came back and couldn't see anyone I opened the door."

He looked up at Paul. He didn't need to spell it out, what he'd witnessed.

"Since arriving here I've seen and done things. Things with girls, you understand. I know you do, you're doing well here. You're popular. But I can't make sense of what I saw. Help me."

"What do you want?" Paul's brain whirred. He had ideas but needed to hear more. How had Mark processed what he saw?

"Is Alton a complete freak? You're normal, I didn't see you doing anything. But what Alton was doing?" Mark was shaking his head and looking genuinely confused. "That was weird."

Anger surged. Paul couldn't hear a word said against Alton but lashing out wouldn't bring about anything positive. And Alton's well being that was Paul's greatest priority.

Thinking fast Paul wondered how this situation might be turned to his benefit? Somehow he suspected confessing his undying love for Alton would not be the best way forward. "So I guess you've not had your dick sucked, yet?" he asked.

"No."

"But you've performed oral sex, on a woman I mean?" Put him on the defensive. Try to make Mark feel foolish and insecure to deflect his bullying attention away from Alton.

"No."

"Sorry, I forget that some people don't progress through ST as fast as others." Undermining Mark's arrogant confidence should help. "Look Alton might be way ahead of you but don't worry about it. You don't have to do anything you don't want to, and I won't mention to anyone that you are worried about little things like that."

Paul turned to leave, indicating the conversation was over and to assert his control over the situation. He wanted to leave Mark confused, but in no doubt that Paul was beyond question, and by association, therefore, so was Alton. That exposing them would backfire on Mark.

"I sleep in the same room as Alton. I shower with him in the morning."

Paul leaned in close, feeling more annoyed. "Don't worry about him. He's not going to suck your dick."

"But you didn't think he was going to suck yours when you went for a massage." As he said the words, the expression on Mark's face changed with a new realization. He took a deep breath, sighed and said, "I thought Alton had taken advantage of you. Got you turned on, perhaps you were imagining a woman from earlier but that isn't how it happened, is it?"

Fuck off, Mark. Paul was completely seething but did not want to reveal his feelings.

"Alton wants to do well here, that's why he has thrown himself into the induction training and doing extra, but sucking your dick is not going to get him anywhere. I can assure you it's not going to happen. Now go to bed; I am." Paul turned and walked away.

His roommates were all asleep when Paul returned. He stripped quietly and slipped into bed but lay awake with his brain on overdrive.

After initially finding it difficult to settle into West Beach without Alton, Paul had eventually made friends and enjoyed all the things that were better about this place compared to his old home. The clothes, the food, even the dormitories. There was the possibility to improve your life through working hard.

Then there was the work. It wasn't too bad. Not having a choice about who you have sex with took some getting used to but Paul had found most of the women were quite pleasant, each in her unique way.

For him to give his best performance, he had to focus on what he liked most about an individual woman. This was not always a physical characteristic although it could be. It wasn't all about physical attraction. He focused on aspects of their personality; perhaps something they talked about or the way they said it. With the limited information, he'd build up an imaginary picture about the lives these women lived.

With his twentieth birthday only a few days away Paul did not dwell on the future but had totally enjoyed living in the present. A present that got much better when Alton arrived. Now Alton was here and messing it up big time. Paul smiled to himself under his covers.

Big time! His hand went to his swelling cock as it usually did when he thought about Alton.

Alton's messed it up, and I am glad. He's come here and reminded me that some things are better than all this.

The attraction Paul felt towards Alton was as great as ever. He had never felt that way about another person.

CHAPTER ELEVEN
Alton

Dressed in her typical all-black uniform, Walsh waited outside their usual room as Alton approached for the afternoon's ST session. When she saw him, she walked along the corridor to meet him.

"We're not going in there this afternoon. Today it's just you and me and we're going out." She was carrying a large, black duffel bag.

"Where to?" Alton walked alongside her as they continued together along the corridor.

"Outside. Out of the unit. I thought we'd go down to the beach; it's a good walk. It might be the last warm day we get as autumn's drawing in, so I have a picnic." Walsh indicated her sizable bag. "I've got towels too if you fancy dipping your feet in the sea."

"Going outside—do you mean without guards?" Alton followed her lead down the stairs; two flights took them to the main lobby where he'd stopped Paul and Zander a few days earlier. She continued out of the door, passing through the outside recreation area.

"Don't worry; you will be quite safe. We are miles from civilization so there shouldn't be anyone else on the beach.

Guards monitor outside the unit, you know. If undetected terrorists are camping out there, I'm armed and I have my martial arts training to fall back on."

"You surprise me. You seem harmless." Alton joked. Walsh looked every bit as tough as any of the guards and she didn't look beach-ready or as if she'd have any interest in paddling.

"Looks can be very deceptive. Don't you already know that?"

They both laughed. Things felt very natural between them as if friendships between men and women were normal.

Alton had warmed to both Walsh and Freya, preferring their company to that of his fellow trainees. They didn't push him into doing anything in the sex training sessions, and they also had made no issue of his lack of progress. They treated him as if it were entirely typical for a man to turn down the chance to touch a naked woman.

But Alton knew his behavior wasn't *normal* because of what the other guys said when they were in a group, not just the new recruits but the mentors too. He was different.

"I wasn't worried about anti-men extremists attacking us; I mean aren't the guards supposed to stop me running away?"

"Yes, that's right. No keeping the matriarchal conspiracy a secret from you, is there?" Walsh raised her eyebrows as she looked him in the face with some surprise.

After more than a moment's silence, Walsh said, "I don't know why you would say such a thing. The guards protect you all so you can have a safe life. Otherwise, you'd all be hunted down by those militant extremists and who knows what."

"They'd wipe out men. Womankind would have to rely on frozen sperm and some other dubious reproduction techniques. Eventually, it would be the end of the human race, I expect. They are a minority, but they're crazy and ruthless."

Men were rare and precious since the pandemic. Very few babies were born and of them very few were male. A minority of women blame men for everything bad in history, including the pandemic itself, and would punish men today for the crimes of their forefathers. That's why males were raised together in safe communities. However, Alton didn't feel precious, he felt miserable.

"Okay. Sorry, no need to get so serious; it was just a joke," he said. "But you've got to admit, with the high walls and security it does look like we're kept in a prison."

"A unit to keep you safe from outsiders, not keep you as prisoners."

Alton wasn't so sure. The unit kept them safe as sex-workers and prisoners. He didn't feel like he had many choices open to him or that he was free to come and go.

They didn't exit by one of the main gates at the front of the building. They walked across the grounds at the back, past the sports' courts and the village. Alton couldn't walk that way without glancing in the direction of Paul's sleeping quarters.

Several hectares of cultivated allotments lay beyond the buildings—some of the men enjoyed recreational gardening and a feast of freshly grown produce made its way to the kitchen and the dining room each day.

A gate through the first perimeter fence led to the attached farm, so far Alton had not left the main compound.

The unit was called West Beach, and he often smelled the salt on the breeze. He knew they were near the sea because of his journey but he had not seen it once since his arrival.

Alton and Walsh were waved through the first gate into the farm and then immediately turned to exit through another gate. Wild grasses grew up a steep slope. They climbed and Alton realized they were on the sand dunes.

"A little steep walking here, then sand dunes, then more sand and then the sea," Walsh commented on their journey. "How does West Beach compare to the Foresters?"

"It's luxury." Alton did not elaborate. He was aware that the questions were probing rather than chit-chat as if this conversation was heading to a particular place as it must be; why else were they out here on the sand?

"Do you like living here?" Continuing with the brisk walk across the rough terrain, Walsh did not look at Alton.

"How couldn't I like it? Who wouldn't like it?" *Where is this going?*

"Then why do you look so anxious all the time?"

"Do I? I didn't know I did." Alton wondered why Walsh was approaching this topic in such an awkward way. It was obvious he wasn't making progress in the ST sessions. "I don't fit in. I don't want to leave, but you'll tell me to go, eventually."

Couldn't she imagine what it was like as a new youth, arriving here and facing failure? Didn't she understand that all the others talked about how much they enjoyed the work, and that just made it all worse? When Alton listened to the conversations of his peers, it reinforced his identity as an outcast.

Walsh turned to look at Alton and seemed genuinely surprised. "Why do you think you'll be told to leave?"

"You have been in the ST lessons with me haven't you?" Alton spat out the words. Why was she getting him to spell it out?

"You've been here little more than a week, and you've not had sex with a woman; that's no big problem."

"I don't want to do it, not now or next week or ever. That is the problem." A nauseous sensation grew, and he became hot and clammy. Things were coming to a head fast. He'd not prepared, and he had no control over the conversation. Just like he had no control over his life.

She took his outburst in her stride, showing no surprise. Perhaps more men complained like this than he realized.

"Don't worry; that is not the only skill valued here."

"Isn't it?" It was Alton's turn to be surprised. "Everyone's said that's the work, and we've all got to do it. I can't do it."

They stood at the brow of a hillock looking over the sand dunes. The flat golden sand stretched for miles further ahead and sunlight glistened off the blue sea on the horizon.

"Having sex with women is not the only important thing that goes on at WB. Look around you." West Beach was already in the distance, hidden behind an imposing wall, in the opposite direction a barrier of sea met the sky and around them the sand dunes blended into the beach.

"I wanted to bring you out here, away from everyone else so we can talk frankly without the fear of being overheard."

There was nobody in sight except for guards in the distance at the perimeter wall.

"There are things you don't know, things that most of the men don't know. If they told you every man has to have sex with women, then that is what they honestly believe, but it isn't true."

Now Walsh had Alton's full attention.

"Most women are not interested in men; there are millions of women in the country, and most don't care if you live or die. As a species we would survive without men. There's plenty of frozen sperm and there are ways to reproduce girl babies just from women. I don't know much about that—I'm not that kind of scientist, but they can do it. That's one of the reasons the anti-men lobby is so strong."

"They blame men for the disaster and everything that was bad before. They don't want society to support men or male communities now. They are gaining support from less militant women who are concerned about the cost of maintaining these units when alternative fertility methods are cheaper, and from women who believe the sex side of the work here is unethical."

Walsh nodded in the direction that they had come. "Now you've found out that a few women, deviants we call them, want to have sex with men as you've seen. But it's taboo. Most women don't, they are asexual."

He noticed her wording. "You're not a deviant?"

She didn't answer. "Deviants are encouraged to have treatment to stop those urges."

You said not all men here have sex with women. Alton wanted to know more about this specifically but didn't want to interrupt.

"We're a community. Men who can't work in one way can still contribute in another and we look after the old and sick. Just as you did at your previous home. Let's review the basics, Alton. Why are you here?"

"I don't know. Why am I here?" he asked.

"All males live in the safety of the men's units, and they are almost all asexual, impotent and infertile. Boys are monitored to see if they might have what it takes to live and work here. You certainly have it, Alton. You're here because you're fertile and although we have well-stocked sperm banks, at some point in the future the supplies may need to be replenished or we may need a greater variation of genetic backgrounds. I'm not that kind of scientist so I don't know too much about it, but that is the primary reason for men to live here. So you are qualified."

It was the first time this had been explained to him. He was here for fertility reasons, not sex, from what she was saying. Walsh continued to look at the view rather than him. She was so casual as if this conversation wasn't a big deal to her.

"At the moment the main income for the unit, for all men's units, is through the sex work that the men do here." It was as if there were two different versions of what was required of him.

"And I don't think I can do that," he said with a big sigh.

"You've been here what, barely a week?" she asked.

"A week in which the ST training has gotten nowhere," he replied.

"On the contrary. In those ST sessions you've spent intimate, social time with a woman, or women if you include me. This is a whole new experience for you."

"What makes you think I can do it?"

"I know you can do it, or you wouldn't be here. Is there a problem with Freya? Isn't she your type?"

How could he tell her Freya wasn't his type? He remained silent.

"What do you think about when you're alone? I know you get turned on but what does it for you?"

"Freya isn't my type," he whispered, then hesitated. Could he tell her? It would have to come out, eventually. "Men. I think about men, not women." Alton mumbled his forced confession, he dreaded the reaction.

Momentarily Walsh looked stunned and then the biggest smile possessed her face.

"You're gay. I thought you might be, but I couldn't assume." She sounded genuinely thrilled. "Do you have a lover? Have you had a lover?"

Alton wasn't sure how much he wanted to share, but he saw no reason to lie. It was a relief to tell her and he was encouraged by her response.

"Yes. Yes."

"I told you a tiny minority of women are deviants who want to have sex with men. I'm not one of them. I don't understand it any more than you do. What you don't know is more women want to watch men have sex with each other. You can do that."

Alton remained quiet.

"Women want it. Will pay well to watch, but we have so few men who are willing to go with men." She put her bag down on the sand where they were standing. "Let's sit down here among the dunes, later we'll dip our toes in the sea."

Alton felt grateful for the opportunity to sit, taking the responsibility away from his shaking legs.

Every day had been full of surprises since he arrived at West Beach less than two weeks ago. He had spent ten days learning about pleasuring women. Now he was told that he did not even need to be doing that.

"So why didn't you tell me that in the first place? Ask me? Why have you been showing me all the stuff so far? It just didn't seem right. I tried, but it wasn't working." The traumatic experience of the past few days bubbled inside him. Why put him through this if they wanted him as he was? A man who liked sex with men.

"I have to teach all newcomers the same. At first, I didn't know for sure how you would turn out. You had the same training as everyone else. When they arrive here at nineteen, men have very limited experience with women. They are usually virgins, but most learn quickly. Perhaps you had sex with a man at the Foresters?"

Alton didn't answer.

"The truth is, and we don't know why, the vast majority of men here are heterosexual. They could put on a show with other guys, but they don't want to when there is plenty of opportunity for sex with different woman."

Walsh got two towels out of the bag and laid them in a slightly shady dip; a palm tree and tall grasses growing on the mound cast some shade. She sat on a towel and Alton did the same.

"Here's something you don't know. Men don't usually talk about what goes on with their clients. There are so few gay or bisexual men but a high demand to watch or join in with them so those are the men at the top of the leaderboard. You could be there too. I have a list of guys you could work with or perhaps you have a secret lover if he isn't already on my list."

She lay back. "Think about it."

"I don't know if my lover is on your list."

"I can't tell you their names but you can tell me his name."

"Paul Knight."

"Pardon."

"Paul Knight. He's my lover. He's the only one I want to do that sort of thing with. I don't know if he's on your list. Is he on your list?"

"I'll be honest with you; Paul is on my team too. I know who he is. But I can't name names from the gay list. I keep those guy's preferences confidential, just as I will about you and Paul."

Sharing personal information liberated Alton from the burden that had been weighing him down over recent days. They lay on the sand in silence for many minutes before a new feeling of outrage began to surface. "You're telling me you want us to perform, just to entertain the audience. You don't care how we feel."

"Calm down, I don't think you understand what I'm saying."

"What don't I understand?"

"Everyone earns an income from their sex work and men who do gay shows are in demand. They earn the most. You see, the guys with the most leisure time, the best rooms, high on the leaderboard, they didn't win by doing the same as everyone else—they made their money from doing something different. Something most men don't want to do or can't do."

"I'm not interested in earning the most money."

"There's no need to be indignant about it. It is this income that pays to run all the men's units, not just this one. Money from sex work here goes to look after young boys at places like The Foresters. Pays for clothes and guards and other stuff. It is just a job and some of those who make money from acting with men aren't gay but good at doing what it takes."

She gave him plenty to think about and Alton remained quiet, listening. "If you do want to stay here, you like the quality of life, and you'd like to be with Paul. It's all possible."

"You thought to survive here guys have to have sex with women; he might think that too. It's wrong, but the culture among the men is..." Walsh paused as if trying to find the right words. "Well, it doesn't matter. I'll talk to Paul about that. The main thing is, you don't have to have sex with women. You can just do shows with men. You can live with Paul as your boyfriend here. It's not against the law or anything. And, if anything, most men will be pleased that you are not competing against them for the female customers."

"I need to think about it."

"Take your time." She nodded. "Let's leave the stuff here and go down to the sea. There's no hurry. I'm here to talk and answer your questions any time. I am your trainer but also please consider me as your friend."

The soft white sand was hot under their bare feet, Walsh had slipped off her shoes and ran to the sea with Alton in pursuit and her gun still in its holster. It was reassuring to know she could still protect them on this apparently isolated beach.

After a light picnic brunch, of tiny cut sandwiches and fruit, Walsh put on her shoes and returned to the main purpose of the day.

"You and Paul could spend time like this on this beach."

"That would be good." Doubt filled his heart. "I don't know what he wants though."

"You can find out. Ask him. I can arrange for you to spend tonight together."

Alton didn't speak but his eyes widened. This was all too good to be true.

"Today there is a party by the pool. Many of our mature, regular ladies are attending. They've all been coming here for at least ten years so they don't mind seeing each other, they respect each other's need for discretion and they like to party with the men outside of the rooms. There's no sex, that's not what I mean; they just socialize, laugh, dance. There will be live music. It will be good fun."

"You and Paul should have some fun together too, dance, and I will arrange for you to have suite number one for the night. Whenever you are ready, just go there. I let the guards know."

"Really?" It sounded too good to be true. Privacy without fear of interruption. Spending hours together, the whole night. "Yes, thanks. Thank you, Walsh." It was so much to take in.

"No. Didn't I already tell you? I'm like you." She smiled and stood up, the session was coming to an end but there was still the walk back to the perimeter wall.

"You mean you like other women? Is that normal?" He was curious but floundering, he knew so little about women and how they lived.

She looked him in the eye. "It's normal for me but no. It's not viewed as normal by most women. We are thought of as deviants too. Out here, most women believe sexual urges are primitive animal instincts, that's all. I'd appreciate it if you'd tell no one."

He felt honored that she'd trusted him with her secret. He didn't know what life was like in female society but he understood the need for secrecy.

"Alton, you and Paul can have the luxury suite tonight. I'll organize it as soon as we get back."

It was with a certain sense of excitement that Alton faced the rest of the day. There was the real possibility that he could make a successful life, a real career, at West Beach. He wasn't sure he wanted to, but it was good to know the possibility was there. A life with Paul, if Paul wanted him.

He wasn't sure what Paul wanted.

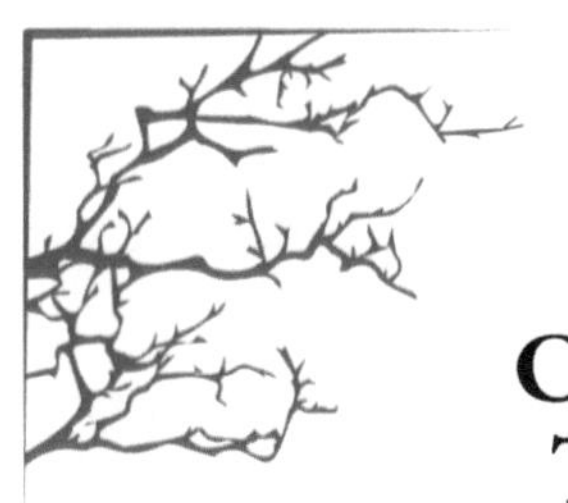

CHAPTER TWELVE
Paul

"Here he comes."

"Here comes a true player!" His teammates sounded delighted to see him as he arrived at the pitchside, just in time.

"Paul, the man we need. Thought you weren't going to make it."

"We're in with a chance now. We'd have been slaughtered on the field, but now we got our newest, youngest, secret weapon."

Paul wasn't the best player, not by a long shot, but good enough that his teammates wanted him.

"Get your kit on. Kick off's in five."

What a day. From a job he had to endure, with a client he could barely tolerate to a position he liked. With great relief after his rough morning, Paul walked out in time to join his team in the tournament.

On the pitch, he had real control over something, for the duration of the match. As a West Beach gigolo, he felt manipulated and used. The work suited some guys, Paul understood that. And some clients weren't so bad. But a morning with Kerry seemed like one ordeal too many.

Both his client and his teammates saw him as a new young man, which he was. Both client and teammates thought he could do something amazing for them. The big difference was how Paul felt about the two.

As a client, Kerry demanded something he couldn't give. She wanted not just his body but an emotional intimacy, too. The team also expected commitment, which he was pleased to give.

He'd forget about everything else as he concentrated on the game. Running swiftly, keeping an eye on his teammates and the opposition. Spotting the gaps and opportunities. It wasn't all about him and what he could do with the ball, but playing as a group. With a strategy. The speed, adrenaline, and concentration would chase the monsters from his mind.

When Paul returned to the pitch in his uniform, the referee and the team captain approached the players. "We're taking five more minutes. Sorry for the delay, lads."

Like a lot of men, Paul isolated himself for these minutes before the start of play. Warm-up exercises weren't just about flexing his body and preparing his muscles for exertion but getting his brain on the game.

She'd said she loved him. She wanted more. She said exclusivity was possible; she could afford it. He'd recoiled and tried to hide his repulsion at the very notion. He went through the motions with her all the while strengthening his resolve to decline her bookings in the future.

He was in love with someone else. It hit him hard at that moment with that client. He didn't want to make her unhappy but how much he wanted to make things right for the person he truly loved.

The rest of the session with Kerry was barely tolerable but with Alton at the front of Paul's mind, he raised the topic of the medication. He was determined to find out what he could in the final encounter with this woman.

Alton might be in the watching crowd, and if he was, then Paul knew where he'd be. He glanced in that direction but couldn't pick out any individuals as he was called to position.

Paul ran out onto the pitch to a few jeers from the other side. Young men weren't seen as an asset in a team. Players were at their peak at eighteen or nineteen at The Foresters, but here the best were five or six years older, well into their twenties. Paul wanted to do well on the pitch at West Beach where he would forget about the clients and enjoy the after match celebrations as part of a triumphant team.

Underdog was not a position he wanted to try. Paul liked winning.

CHAPTER THIRTEEN
Alton

Struggling to get his mind around the facts, Alton couldn't keep the silly grin off his face. Sex with women was not a prerequisite to living at West Beach. A burden lifted from his shoulders, the prospects for his future much improved after just one frank conversation and one trip to the beach.

He had no idea what Paul wanted from him—with him—but at least they had options he never before thought possible. They could be valued members of the community without doing that work.

Amazingly, they could be role models, up there on the leaderboard as big earners. Alton knew that would appeal to Paul. The younger boys at The Foresters admired Paul and followed him as a leader; even the older men held him in high regard and Paul was naturally made for the role. Alton didn't have such lofty ambitions to achieve high status but he would welcome respect from his fellow men.

The next day was Paul's birthday, and Alton wanted to give a gift to remember. He imagined how the night might play out.

Paul would appear, walk boldly up to Alton and kiss him on the lips, in front of everyone, leaving all the surrounding men speechless as they watched the lingering kiss. After they prised themselves apart, Alton and Paul would walk away, arm in arm, disappearing to a private room where they would hold each other close all night long.

Then again perhaps it wouldn't go like that.

Discretion might be wiser, maintaining their secret as they always had done. Not everyone needed to know and there were benefits to being part of a tiny conspiracy.

When Alton and Paul gazed lovingly at each other across a crowded room, no-one else knew what those eyes were saying to each other. The perfect conclusion to any scenario involved undressing each other in privacy and holding each other close all night long.

In preparation for the evening and night ahead, Alton decided to visit the Wardrobe Masters.

"Well hello, handsome," Philip was all smiles as he jumped up from a sewing machine when Alton entered. "Well, you look like the cat who's got the cream. What's up with you?"

"Nothing," Alton snapped, a little too defensively. "Where's Steven?"

"We don't get locked in here! He's having some time out for good behavior, so it's just me holding the fort. Can I help you?"

"Yes, I'm sure you can. I've not been here long, and you've sorted me out some great clothes, but I'm just not used to, you know, wearing new clothes. It sounds bad, doesn't it?"

"Believe me, darling, you sound completely mad, but you're cute enough to get away with it."

Philip, you are a flirt.

"I remember on my first day here you promised to make me look good enough to eat, and I want to look that good tonight. What should I wear?"

"Interesting problem, and I'm so pleased you've come to me. You're asking the right man. But first you have to tell me, I'm fairly sure that you're not dressing up for the benefit of a client?"

"How do you know?"

"You've not been here two weeks. Even if you had a booking with a client, very few young men worry about what they are going to wear until they've had far more experience. So, my guess is you want to attract the attention of either a man or."

"Or?"

"Don't tell me it's a guard."

"I won't."

"I knew it!" Philip clasped his hands to his gleeful looking face. "I said to Steven, after you came back the second time, that I liked you."

It was Alton's turn to stare silently.

"Oh, I don't mean like that. You are easy on the eyes. I just mean, I thought you might be one of us. Anyway, this man you want to impress, does he know about you?"

Alton relaxed. He'd found someone else to talk with about his relationship. Blushing, with a smile he replied, "Yes he knows. He knows I like him and he's into me too. I'm not sure how serious he is but I'm hoping to get some answers out of him tonight."

"The two of you will have friends and support in us. We're always here if you need us. Not just for clothes but to talk or hang out together as the select group of guys who like guys."

"Thanks. That's good to know. I'm not going to tell you who he is. If he wants it to stay a secret, so be it. But I hope I'll be able to tell you when I see you next."

"My advice to you would be to respect and keep these secrets. If I told you how long I've been here that would reveal my age, so let me just say, I've been here a long time and being different can make you unpopular. It can be best if you don't stand out too much."

"Thanks."

"Now, let's talk clothes. I am picturing, tight vest or T-shirt to show off your assets. You don't work so hard in the gym to hide that chest away."

The young crowd was in the usual place by the pool that evening, but no sign of Paul.

Alton kept a watchful eye out for him. Walsh assured him Paul would not be working. If he had to, Alton would resort to searching for him and not giving up even if it meant dragging him out of his cabin at bedtime. Paul didn't know about the room available just for them, just for tonight, but there was no way Alton intended to miss out on that opportunity.

Alton was excited to see Paul and couldn't wait to spend leisurely hours with him instead of a few furtive stolen moments.

Finally, at long last, Paul appeared in the crowd. Time for the daydreaming to end and the real dream to play out. Wow! Paul looked hot. Dressed head to toes in crisp black clothes,

T-shirt, jeans, and boots. He looked around the crowd, and quickly his eyes rested on Alton.

There was no mistaking the way Paul bit his bottom lip as he eyed Alton up and down.

Alton kept looking straight back at him; he knew he looked good, in his tight white jeans and skimpy tight white vest. *Thank you, Wardrobe Master!* Alton looked powerful and oozed the sort of confidence that came from feeling good about himself and knowing the man he loved wanted him as bad as he wanted him. No hurry, though.

The E12 roommates were all together, they were laughing and chatting. Paul walked away from his friends without comment, as soon as he noticed Alton, losing no time in coming directly over to him. He walked right up to Alton, into his personal space and far closer than necessary, almost touching but not quite.

In a low voice, Paul said, "Did you know it's my birthday tomorrow?"

Alton felt self-conscious. If anyone was to look their way, they were standing far too close together, face to face. Almost as if from his fantasy. But this was Paul's decision; Paul had come this close. Paul mustn't care what people thought.

"Of course, I remember your birthday. And I have an amazing present for you."

"You do?" Paul raised his eyebrows in surprise. "It's my birthday tomorrow, and I know how I'd like to spend it."

Something fluttered inside Alton. In public, he wasn't expecting such aggressive flirting, and he liked it.

"We could go now, or we stay and mingle a little first," Alton suggested without telling Paul where they were going.

"I've been mingling here for months; I don't want to wait any longer. I'm ready to go anywhere with you."

"Let's go inside then."

Without stopping to speak to anyone, Alton led the way inside knowing Paul was admiring him from behind. No one paid them any attention except Mark; he seemed to be glaring at them.

As soon as they were inside the main building, out of sight of the crowd but not exactly hidden from public view, Paul put his hand into Alton's and asked, "Where to now? Not the gym!"

"No, not that again. I have a present. A room pass from Walsh. And we've got all night."

CHAPTER FOURTEEN
Paul

Disappearing from the party within minutes of arriving was not something Paul had planned, but just lately nothing went to plan. He should give up on planning.

Yet again, he'd returned an impressive performance on the sports field. His team was well ahead in the tournament and the players were treated like heroes for the day. In addition, he'd done his work. He'd suffered the client and done chores. He'd damn well earned his right to enjoy relaxation time in the way he wanted.

Paul deserved to spend time with Alton and to hell what anyone else thought. The man he loved to talk to, flirt with, and so much more.

It had been a tough few days for Alton, and Paul wanted to give support, to show Alton how much he cared. He loved Alton and had nothing to hide. He'd tell his roommates soon, after discussing it with Alton, if they didn't hear something from Mark first.

He had walked to the party at the recreation area with Jay and a crowd of men from the village. Zander and Rayfe had already gone ahead to ready their instruments for later performances.

As soon as he saw him, Paul approached Alton as planned.

Paul hadn't factored in that gorgeous, sexy Alton, in person, took his breath away and made him so goddamn horny. As soon as he spotted Alton, rational thoughts left his mind. Paul was torn between ravishing him in public or whisking him away for sex, but Alton led them away from the recreation area, and Paul thought he might be blushing due to the thoughts racing through his mind. He was certainly hot and bothered.

He was taken by surprise when Alton said he had a room. How did that happen?

"I'll explain later, we've got all night."

The finest luxury suite in West Beach awaited them. Unfortunately, Paul had been here only days before; he shuddered, trying to shut that memory out. He understood why Alton wanted to explore, inspecting everything as he examined all the finery. There were mirrors everywhere. They could watch themselves from every angle. Lights, lamps, ornaments, decorative details. The room just seemed so busy compared to anything they were used to.

Paul grabbed him around the waist from behind and pressed his groin against Alton's ass. "I know you want to investigate but we've got all night, you said it yourself. And I've got something here that can't wait."

Alton swiveled to face Paul with sheer delight on his face. "And what would that be?"

"I can't wait all night to fuck you. I need you on my cock."

Paul wanted to have the leisurely sex that he remembered they used to have. Sex in every position with endless hours for pleasure. At their previous home, they would find the space and time to fuck most days. Totally different to the few times they'd come together here.

"Me too. It's been a very long time." This wasn't the same stressed man from the gym. A transformation. Whatever had happened, Alton was happy and relaxed.

"You sure we got all night?" Paul asked.

"Definitely." Alton nodded enthusiastically.

"Time for more than once then."

"Yes, definitely." Alton's gray eyes sparkled.

Taking several deep breaths, trying to remain calm Paul let go of Alton and removed his clothes while Alton did the same. Of all the men he'd ever met, including some very cute ones, Paul marveled at how much he wanted to touch Alton; he was so very attractive.

Over recent months, Paul had come to terms with the fact that he found men attractive, in general, far more than he was interested in women. But what amazed him was how much more attracted he was to Alton, in particular, much more than any other man. It was a combination of Alton's body and his personality.

Alton's physique was muscular, of course, and the top he was wearing now didn't cover much. It was great to spend some time admiring the body that he wanted to touch and hold for the rest of the night. And every night after that.

Alton slipped off his shoes, his white jeans, and underwear. He stood in front of Paul looking exquisite.

"Stay there. I want to admire you."

Alton stood still, naked, ripped with definition. Broad shoulders wrapped in taut, soft skin. Not much body hair. A semi-erection, pointing out from a thatch of short curls.

Paul stepped towards Alton, placed a flat palm on the strong, washboard stomach. Pacing slowly, he circled Alton moving his hands around his waist but dipping and rising slightly to trace the man's skin over toned muscles, across his chest, back and rear. Behind him, he ran his fingers along the crack of Alton's ass.

Alton shuddered.

Soon. There would be plenty of time to caress every inch as the night went on.

Paul continued to the front of Alton and moved so close to him that they melded together as one as they kissed. The first kiss of the day. Despite the longing between them and the firmness of their dicks pressed together, the kiss was soft and tender.

"I didn't imagine a day like this," Paul said when their lips parted.

"What 'like this' do you mean?" Alton asked.

"Perfect. Having you for the whole night, no hurry, no sneaking around, no worrying about being caught. We haven't fucked in months, and I want you so much. I feel desperate enough that we should have already done it! And now we're here naked and just kissing not fucking it's surreal."

"Well, I haven't had sex with anyone but you so if someone is desperate, I am. Can we get on with it?"

They chuckled.

"Sometimes I love the way you seduce me," Paul joked, and they both laughed. Holding hands, they clambered onto the bed, both kneeling, facing each other and kissing. Paul lowered Alton gently onto his back.

He buried his face into his lover's blond hair, tickling his ear with his tongue and savoring the smell of him. Familiar. A smell he'd known all his life and could conjure up in his head.

A smell that stopped him getting too close to the female partners as no one else smelled like Alton. A smell that both turned him on and made him feel at home.

"I can't tell you how much I've missed you and how much I wanted this day to happen." On his back, Alton wrapped his legs around Paul.

Paul tried to remain in control. The past few days at West Beach just kept getting better. Alton, appearing out of the blue. Alton, lying in his bed. Alton, getting along with his roommates. And now this. On top of Alton and about to fuck him.

He moved his head from Alton's hair; he would visit this place again later.

They had all night.

"What do you want, Alton? You arranged this; what do you want us to do?"

"You know what I want. Stop messing with me."

Paul knew all right.

He reached out, grabbed the lube from the side of the bed and wriggled down the bed between Alton's legs. Pausing only for a second to admire the delicious cock. He brought his mouth down to meet his lover's balls. Licking and kissing, he headed south from there over the soft, smooth, sensitive place before working his tongue along the crack of his ass. He lapped and probed the hole with his wet tongue and enjoyed Alton's response. It had been months since they'd done this; no wonder Alton was so eager, so responsive.

He warmed some lube in his hand while pleasuring with his tongue and then carefully inserted a finger, pushing beyond the initial resistance.

Alton gasped.

Paul eased the digit in and withdrew it, almost out, repeating the movement a few times before doubling up and continuing with the motion with two fingers.

"Do it, Paul. Stop teasing and fuck me."

Happy to oblige, Paul raised himself into position.

What about a condom? Paul used condoms with clients, but they didn't have them at The Foresters. He'd never heard of them before arriving here. Alton wouldn't expect a condom.

Similarly with lube. The boys discovered a new use for oil appropriated from the kitchen at The Foresters; here it was available by the bed. He wiped a little extra lube on his dick before penetrating Alton's defenses.

Reveling in the tight and hot squeeze of his cock, moving in and out slowly, he was thankful again that they had all night as he was quite sure he wasn't going to last long this time. His whole body was readying for orgasm, whether he wanted it or not. He did. His eyes swept up and down, from Alton's face, eyes staring back at him, to his still hard cock that Alton was now grasping.

Paul lowered his body so they could kiss.

"Alton."

"Yes, Paul."

"We've definitely got all night?"

"Yes, Paul."

"Good. I want you on your knees later."

Alton whimpered.

"Alton, I've got to come." His balls tightened, his voice a little strained, the words difficult to get out. He was at the very edge the next moment when the wet splatter of Alton's cream dotted his chest. There was no stopping Paul's orgasm as his body spasmed and his seed pumped through his pulsating cock into Alton's ass.

For a moment the world stopped as he shuddered and heat consumed his being.

As he came back to consciousness, Paul saw Alton's eyes were moist and, if he wasn't mistaken, a stray tear was rolling back, pulled by gravity, towards his ear.6y4ywould do anything to make things right.

"Nothing's wrong. It's so right. I'm so happy." Alton sniffed. "I have something to tell you. I was going to wait, but I can tell you now."

"I'm listening." Paul had things he wanted to tell Alton too but he could wait.

"Get off, first, before you squash me."

Paul rolled off and ran his hand over Alton's chest, fingering the drying semen. "We keep talking about talking," he said.

Alton added, "But not actually talking. We will now, soon, but let's shower first."

The shower room was large and luxurious. The floor and walls covered in large, shiny, ceramic tiles. A whole team of guys could clean up under the numerous powerful jets that sprayed from the ceiling and one wall. The floor gently sloped toward a single drain.

The men rubbed soap and water over each other in between lingering wet kisses. They were in the shower long enough for their dicks to make a full recovery and return to their hard and upright former glory as they crashed and rubbed together.

The men cleaned themselves, dried up and still slightly damp they slipped naked between the sheets. Cuddling and their legs entwined together, they didn't care about their wet hair saturating the pillows.

"Why were you crying?" asked Paul.

"I don't know what's wrong with me. It's just such a relief. It's been so stressful. When you left, I thought I'd never see you again. Then when I got here, I've been here less than two weeks, and I thought they'd send me away. And we really wouldn't see each other again."

Paul was confused. "Why would they send you away?"

"I'm not like you Paul. I can't do it with women."

This made things no clearer.

Alton explained. He briefly told him about the ST sessions and the conversation with Walsh on the beach. His concerns and her suggestion.

The information amazed Paul. "I had no idea that was an option. In my months here no one's ever mentioned it."

"Well, I guess you've been passing okay as straight, so far."

"I could have only got away with it for so long. By which I mean not much longer." They both laughed at this.

"Alton, I've only been thinking about you too. I was confused by it all when I first got here. Obviously, I've serviced the clients, it was novel at first and I'm always up for trying new things. Over time, the acting has become increasingly difficult. I can do it but the truth is, I don't fancy the women either."

Paul wondered what he would have done if Alton hadn't turned up here? From what Walsh had said, there were others like them, maybe tens or perhaps hundreds;

"What next? When we leave this room tomorrow?"

"Tomorrow I'm still on induction, and you still have your job, and your room in E12 but I guess Walsh will tell me how we fit into what she has in mind." Alton seemed so much more sure of himself and his place here at West Beach.

Paul grinned. "It could be a lot of fun. Just you and me together, women watching us. Getting paid to do what we want to do together anyway."

"Yeah. Just think it could a whole new sexual adventure." Alton cocked his head to one side. "And what about that thing she mentioned about being involved with other people too?"

"If you want to. I'm just so happy being with you." Paul had had enough of other people, for the time being, but understood that Alton hadn't had that experience.

Alton said, "If my best friend were with me perhaps I might enjoy it, new people and experiences." He had a cheeky look on his face and a twinkle in his eyes.

CHAPTER FIFTEEN
Paul

As soon as he'd finished performing in the recreation area, still holding his guitar by its neck, Rayfe marched directly to Paul, who was sitting with a crowd of men.

Rayfe's Spanish guitar sessions were among the most popular of all the music at West Beach. Indeed, being exceptional musicians was something three of the E12 residents had in common though they all played different styles and so rarely performed together.

Paul was very much the odd one out among his roommates, as a non-musician, but he excelled at track sports. His previous community prized hunting skills more highly than music.

"Paul, can I have a word?"

Paul stood up immediately, "Yes. Is something the matter?"

"I'm not sure. Let's go to E12 now and talk before the others get back. I'll just get the guitar case." The others referred to were Jay and Zander, of course. They were both with clients.

Paul said a swift farewell to the surrounding youths, including Alton, and left with Rayfe.

"Want to give me a clue what it's all about?"

"It's something Mia told me." It was no secret among the E12 team that Rayfe and Mia had romantic feelings for each other that went beyond a client and gigolo relationship.

It made Paul feel a little alarmed. Not that he wasn't happy for Rayfe. Rayfe was in love, and Paul was very pleased things were working out well for him. But he worried that Kerry wanted the same, or that any other client would want that bond with him. A bond he had with someone already.

"I just saw Mia a little earlier today before the evening jam and, to be honest, I just wanted to talk to you about it straight away." They both focused on the path ahead. Once night fell there was little light to illuminate the route.

When they arrived at their cabin, they entered in silence and Paul took a seat at the table while Rayfe kicked off his shoes and slouched on his bed.

"Paul, is there something you've not been telling us?"

"I have no idea, what about?" There were many things.

It was just a matter of time before Mark revealed what he'd seen. Paul was surprised it hadn't come out already.

After their all-night session, a few days ago, they decided to tell no one for a while. They wanted to find out more from Walsh about how things could work out. Mia wouldn't know anything about Alton and him.

"Something about you and Jay, perhaps?"

Paul was mystified. "No, I honestly don't know what you're talking about."

"Like having sex with him and making films?"

"We've done threesomes and more. You know that. You were at one of them. But I don't know anything about films."

"I don't mean threesomes. I mean just you and Jay in a twosome? I've seen you guys flirting, and I assumed it was just banter, just fun, but now I'm wondering."

Paul couldn't help feeling his skin flush with embarrassment. Paul certainly found Jay attractive much as he tried to hide it. There was that one time with Jay, just before Alton showed up, Paul thought back to the session only a couple of weeks previous. The last session he'd done with his blond roommate. He wasn't ready to kiss and tell, and it was only a little more than kissing because that's what the client wanted. It wasn't a twosome but a threesome.

"What are you talking about, Ray?"

"You remember you've met Mia?"

"Yes, a couple of months ago."

"It wasn't that long ago."

"It just seems like it. Anything beyond two weeks ago seems like a lifetime away." Because that's when Alton showed up.

"She remembers you clearly. And she was very surprised to see a film clip of you and another guy. She didn't know the other guy—she just said he was young and blond—so I thought of Jay. She hasn't met him."

"How did she see this?"

"It was by chance, she said; she went to talk to someone who runs a deviant cinema night. She walked in when the woman was editing a film ready for screening. She told Mia it was newly discovered archive footage from before the pandemic."

"That sounds reasonable. I don't think they can still make films now. All the cameras and stuff stopped working decades ago."

"I thought so too, but Mia has met you and she's certain it was you in the film."

Paul shook his head. "She's mistaken. Maybe it was my great-grandad when he was young."

"Not been making films then, that you know of? What about fucking a blond guy? Because that's what she saw."

Paul was seriously confused. He gulped and his cheeks started to heat up. What he'd done with Jay was minimal, nice but hardly enough to make a film. A little kissing and stuff was what the client wanted to see, but no fucking.

"Fucking then. Not kissing?" Paul was glad he was sitting down as his legs weakened.

"Do you want me to draw a picture?" Rayfe looked slightly amused. "Look, I'm not going to judge you. I don't care if you fuck guys but it is important for us to know if we're being filmed."

Paul felt sick. He wasn't ready for this. He'd planned to tell Ray and the guys in his own time. "What's going on, mate?"

"Mia's had suspicions for quite a while. She thinks they listen in to our conversations.

Paul looked around.

"Not here. We erected these sheds ourselves—there were no hidden wires. But up in the old building, Mia thinks it's wired for spying. She said she was suspicious about the sexy films shown at the club but had no evidence. Then it was pure fluke that she saw this brief clip and recognized you. She says they might do covert filming here. So I wondered if you knew about it. Perhaps it wasn't covert, perhaps you agreed to it? Or it was covert, and you didn't know they'd film you with another dude."

"No, I didn't agree to make a film. What makes her think we're spied on?"

"She doesn't know for sure. A few months ago she was called to meet the Governor to talk about something to do with her work, right after telling me about it."

"Mia met Governor Setchell?"

"Yes. She's met her quite a few times. She hasn't told me details, but she says she suspected Setchell had information that she could only get from someone listening in to our private conversations in the rooms."

"You're telling me Mia thinks we're being spied on when we're with clients? Listened to and filmed without us knowing about it?"

"Yes. That's exactly it. Up in the rooms. She was also amazed by the filming. I got to tell you the film is described as a gay romance, love-thing."

Paul knew Rayfe was examining him and noticed his guilty expression and blushing skin.

"So you must be really into the guy. Are you gonna tell me who it is?"

They sat in silence for a while. Paul weighed up the options and consequences. It would be a relief to share how he felt about Alton with someone, as he'd never talked about it at all. Ever. Until this week. And that had only been with Alton. He wanted to make a life with Alton, a commitment, so telling a few people like his roommates made sense.

"It was you, wasn't it?" Rayfe asked after a while.

He seemed perfectly happy to accept that Paul had a male lover; he was talking as if it were no big deal, just as he had when they discussed Philip and Steven.

"Yes. I don't know about the film but yes, there is a man. I was going to tell you soon."

Rayfe looked a little smug to find out this tidbit. "So, if it's not Jay, who is it?"

"I'm seeing Alton. Like you and Mia."

It was Rayfe's turn to look surprised. "Like Mia and I, huh? You guys are really into each other, then?"

"Yeah. We are." Paul smiled with the relief of sharing this information about himself. "If what you're saying is true, then we were set up by Walsh. The whole encounter was set up by Walsh. She arranged for us to have the room for a night a few nights ago."

"Walsh, huh. Interesting. Mia has her doubts about Walsh too."

"Why? Didn't Walsh help the two of you spend more time together?" Paul was surprised to hear any man casting doubt over their Matriarch's good intentions.

"She did. Just like she got you boys together. You have to wonder what she's doing it for. Mia suspects Walsh and Setchell are in cahoots and it's for their own benefit, not ours. No evidence though. So which room was it?"

"The executive suite." Paul grinned and felt his skin flush as he vividly recalled the events of the night.

Rayfe chuckled as if reading his mind. "Very nice. I wouldn't mind a night in there with Mia."

"Not if there's secret filming going on. I wonder how they do it. It never crossed my mind that it was anything other than..." He floundered seeking the right word and blushed as he recalled that sleepless, exhausting night. He was fit for nothing the next day.

"Look, mate, I don't know what to say about this, but it may be a good thing."

"How? Where do you get that?"

"Well, if there is an audience willing to watch films of the two of you together, then there's a good chance you have a future here working together. They aren't going to make you leave. Remember I told you about Philip and Steven."

"They make a contribution to the community."

"We all do and you and Alton can too. You're lucky. He's here. You can see each other almost any time. Not like Mia and I." Rayfe found it difficult having romantic feelings for Mia when he couldn't act on impulse. Couldn't contact her or visit her or socialize with her outside of WB. To most of the men at West Beach women were only consumers of a service. Fortunately for Rayfe, at least his feelings for Mia were reciprocated.

"I understand that, but we have to keep our relationship secret."

"That's because you've chosen to keep it secret," replied Rayfe. "You don't have to. It doesn't bother me who you love and probably most of the guys wouldn't care either."

Paul was preparing to protest, pointing out everything

"Does anyone else know about the two of you?"

"Just this one guy called Mark, as far as I know. He's a new guy still on induction and a real jerk toward Alton."

"How does he know?"

"Ah."

"He caught you at it?"

"Yeah, he did. And I don't want guys to be mean to Alton."

"Don't worry about it. Most men will treat him fine."

"I'm not sure about that."

Rayfe himself had told them about the hostility toward the other gay couple at West Beach and Paul had seen open hostility.

"Calm down. You've seen how poorly some people behave, but they are a minority. You'll be fine whatever you choose to do. Come out with a celebration party or keep it on the down low. Are you going to tell Jay and Zee? I need to warn them about the illicit filming, but I can do it without mentioning you, if you prefer."

"I'd rather just tell them, as soon as they get back, so it's done. I was going to tell you all, anyway."

After a few moments of silence, Rayfe got up off the bed and picked up his guitar. He pulled a chair away from the table, sat down and began to strum. After sharing a room with three musicians, it did seem the guitar was the most versatile and practical instrument.

Paul appreciated the musical accompaniment to his thoughts. What would he say to the other two?

In the past few months that he had shared a room with them, they had fast become like a family to him, in a way that he never experienced at The Foresters, except with Alton. The four of them had sat up through late nights, sharing confidences, fears, funny stories and true confessions. But there were some things Paul had never shared, until now. Would they take it as another talking point or would they believe he'd lied to them?

Rayfe stopped strumming at the sound of movement outside, and they listened, but the footsteps continued past.

"Mentioning Alton has reminded me of something. I must tell him when I see him." Rayfe continued to play a tune gently while speaking.

"What is it?" Paul was curious.

"I asked Mia about the medicine. You remember Alton was asking about it. I don't recall anyone talking about it since I've been here. It's as if we get here, discover sex and forget all about the old life."

"True. What did she say?" Paul asked.

"It was strange. Firstly, I found out that women don't take medicine all their lives, not even as children, and she says a virus caused the pandemic seventy years ago, but we don't have the virus now. At the time it altered humans forever, DNA she called it. But the point is we were changed as a species; it is passed down to us. We aren't born with a curable illness."

Paul held his hands up. "I don't understand."

"I've only got this because she drew pictures. It's her job, I think. Anyway, she struggled to understand what I was telling her. She had no idea we took medication every day in the other units, and she doesn't know what it's for. She suggested I must have it wrong, that we might have taken it for some other reason."

"That's weird." Paul's brow furrowed.

"Yes, I thought so too," Rayfe agreed.

"What did she think?"

"She just said I had my facts confused."

"I asked Kerry, too." Paul had forgotten about it as so much had happened in the few days since he last saw his science-minded client. "She didn't say much but what was more puzzling was the way she talked. She didn't want to talk about it, and I got the impression she knew more but didn't want to tell me."

They both fell silent as they heard a crowd of voices approaching.

"Sounds like home time." Rayfe focused again on his fingers working the frets of his instrument and he plucked a tune.

Paul, who had relaxed a little while talking, tensed in anticipation of the conversation they were about to have.

Jay burst through the door followed by Zander, and they heard the rest of the crowd disperse to other chalets.

After allowing a few minutes for the men to settle in but before they got ready for bed, Paul wanted to stand up as seemed appropriate for an important announcement, but he feared his legs would give way, and they'd see his hands shaking.

"I have got something to tell you, Zee, Jay." Paul spoke from the same seated position.

They looked at him.

Best to just get it out. "I'm into men more than women." He wanted to pause and let the information sink in but couldn't stop the words flowing. "A few days ago when I was out all night, I wasn't with a client. I spent the night with a man."

"That's why you've been acting strange since then. I thought you were just exhausted after your all-night session." Jay leaned forward eager for the story.

Paul grinned. "I was exhausted after my all-nighter."

"And I'm almost speechless. Don't worry, I said almost!" Jay grinned and glanced around at all the men before focusing back on Paul. "So tell us more. Who is your mystery man?"

"I was with Alton all night. We are lovers."

"When did you get together?" asked Zander.

"We have been together for years." For a moment in the silence that followed Paul wondered if he had done the right thing in confessing something that had been a secret for so long.

Jay was wide-eyed, open mouthed, and speechless.

"That's great Paul; Alton seems nice." Zander was the first to break the silence.

"I'm pleased for you too; you're happy, and Alton's a great guy." Jay agreed. "Just to be clear, are you telling us you guys are in love? And you do kissing and stuff?" His hand shifted to his groin to indicate the sort of stuff he had on his mind.

All eyes were on Paul; even Rayfe looked up though he continued the music. They were waiting for an answer.

Paul nodded, sure he was blushing. He was starting to feel warm and embarrassed. "Yes. What else do you want to ask me?" It was sure to be full of details. That's Jay's style.

Fortunately, Jay didn't get to ask. "Does anyone else know? Do you know how it will affect work or if the powers that be have anything to say about that sort of fraternization?" asked Zander.

"This is the other thing I wanted to talk about."

He explained about the conversation between Walsh and Alton. About how the men could work together offering a different sort of service for the entertainment of the female clients.

He didn't tell them about the conversations he'd had with Rayfe before Zander and Jay arrived. About the suspicion of the use of surveillance technology. He'd leave that to Rayfe. It was notable, however, that Walsh had taken Alton away from the unit, out onto the sandy beach, away from prying ears.

He looked at Rayfe. A coincidence perhaps, or an area free of surveillance.

"I don't believe you," said Jay. "Women are fighting to book repeat sessions with you, and you have the best-looking boyfriend ever."

"I like him, and I'd be happy for him to move in here when he's finished the induction," said Rayfe.

"There are two spare beds, but no keeping the rest of us awake all night with noisy shagging," Zander added, "I don't want to see it."

"Speak for yourself, Zander-the-sensible. No wonder women would pay to watch that. Hell, I'd pay to watch you two too. It'd be hot. Alton is seriously hot."

"Are you saying my boyfriend is hot but I'm not?" Paul teased.

"I just don't think of you like that," Jay replied.

"That's a shame."

"Are you into men as well, Jay?" asked Rayfe.

"No. I don't think so. Well, I don't know. I've never thought about it until just now when Paul said him and Alton..." Jay rubbed at his crotch. "What is it the two of you do?"

"Ask me another time. Best when Alton's around and we'll show you." Paul grinned, this conversation was going down the path of ridiculous.

"Serious, are you okay, Paul?" asked Zander.

"Yeah. It's always been a secret. Our secret for years. I've never told anyone until now, and I don't know what to say." Paul felt genuinely surprised at how well the information was received.

"We four in this room are like a family of brothers. When Alton was here the other night, he fit right in." Rayfe plucked at the strings on his guitar.

"You know this, even though you were asleep?"

"I was resting my body," Rayfe retorted. "Anyway, better to have Alton in one of the spare beds and not someone who doesn't fit in with us. And I don't want Paul to leave just to share a room with Alton."

Paul thought about how he and Alton used to share a bed at The Foresters; he'd like to do that again, but they had a legitimate reason as children in the cold winter. It had possibly not occurred to the men that just having someone close in your bed all night felt good.

"I am all for helping the course of true love. Even if it is between two dudes," Rayfe added. Rayfe had only recently overcome difficulties of his own involving affairs of the heart, in fact, he was still dealing with the difficulties of being in love with a woman in a segregated society, so it was no wonder he was supportive.

"Thanks, mate, " Paul whispered.

"Looks like Alton gets no say in this," said Jay. "In all seriousness, we can just get into the habit of knocking before we barge in here just in case you two are canoodling."

"Is that what we walked in on the other night?" Zander asked.

"Not exactly." Paul's face heated with a blush again, but he wasn't too shy to admit. "We were all done with it by the time you got here."

"Yes!"

The room erupted into whoops and fists in the air.

"Good for you."

"To think, romance has been blossoming right here under my roof, and I almost missed it," Rayfe said.

You did miss it.

Rayfe was about to open the door and stride into the cabin he called home, just as he usually did but, with hand outstretched, he paused. After the recent revelation that one of his roommates preferred boys, he decided to knock. There were some things he didn't want to walk in on.

"Come in." The sound of Zander's voice came from inside E12.

All three roommates were sitting on their beds reading.

Rayfe collapsed onto his bed ready for a nap after his afternoon's workout before heading off to dinner. With his eyes shut he heard Paul striking up a conversation.

"This is pretty rare isn't it?"

"What?" Rayfe asked.

"All of us with nothing to do for a few minutes."

"That's what it's like when protestors stop the clients coming in. It doesn't happen often though."

"This isn't doing nothing; I've wanted to read this for ages," Zander replied. "I thought I'd get some quiet time here in the afternoon."

"And I'm not doing nothing," mumbled Rayfe. "I've been working out."

"Exactly my point," Paul was emphatic. "You wanted to read that book but haven't had the time. How often do we all have the time to sit around doing whatever we want?"

Jay climbed down off his top bunk and sat on a chair. Being above Paul, he couldn't see him, and it was strange having conversations with a disembodied voice.

"There's plenty of time to do whatever I want, but I'm mostly too exhausted to read when we get back here," Zander continued. "What with chores and work and music and sport."

"Is there plenty of free time?" Paul insisted.

"What's your point?" asked Jay.

"Our time is filled with activities. Work, sports, and social activities. It is mostly good, but it leaves us with no spare time, and it means when our time isn't taken up with activities we are too tired to do much else."

"Ah. I see. This is your issue, Paul; it doesn't affect the rest of us. You want more time to spend with lover boy but as we aren't interested in boys, we don't need any more spare time," Zander said.

The others smiled in agreement.

"Yes. You've got a love interest this side of the wall but as we haven't, what would we want downtime for?" Jay asked. "I like the fact that there is plenty to do. It's all fun stuff and much better than the hours of tedious monotony at the units where we all came from."

"Listen," Paul's voice changed to a whisper. "Don't you ever stop to consider how we live like prisoners? And our time is filled up with stuff to keep us too tired to rebel? To keep us from even thinking and questioning."

"You're crazy! What do you think, Zee?"

Without opening his eyes Rayfe joined in the conversation, "Paul has a point."

"What?" Jay exclaimed.

"Why shouldn't Paul and Alton get time alone? Also, why shouldn't I get to spend more time with Mia? Or you get to see Steph or whatever flavor of the month you want, when you choose? Why wait for women to book time with you if and when they can afford it? You'd be happy to see them for free wouldn't you Jay?"

"You're damn right."

"If we were free, we'd spend as much time as we wanted with the ones we love," said Rayfe.

"I'm already getting all the loving I can handle," said Jay.

Zander got off his bed and sat at the table. "I understand. It's not about sex, Jay. It's about having real freedom to choose how we spend our time." Turning to Paul, he said, "You had loads of free time at The Foresters before you came here, we all did, and none of us would like to go back to those units."

"True. Free time meant boredom and living in poverty, rags for clothes, gruel for food," said Jay.

Zander continued, "And when I talk to the women who visit here, I'm not sure that they have much freedom. They work long hours, with a tough life out there. We work shorter hours and the money we make pays for food and clothes, and luxury goods brought in. It paid for these new dorms and the new beds."

"I don't think there's any possible complaint about our quality of life here," said Rayfe. "Paul's talking about the lack of personal freedom. Is that right?"

"Yes, the lack of control. I am wondering if we're not slaves. Imprisoned. Okay, well-looked-after slaves, in a very nice prison but still the same thing."

"So do you have a plan?" asked Zander.

"No." Paul shook his head and smiled. "Not yet."

"Let me know when you do. You could tempt me to escape in search of a better life," Rayfe said.

"You sure?" Jay looked surprised.

"No, I'm not sure. But I would like to be able to go to sleep with Mia in my arms, and spend the whole night with her. Wake up with her and eat breakfast together. And." Rayfe paused for dramatic effect. "Speaking of true love, when is Alton moving in?"

"Tomorrow morning this will officially become his new address." He had unofficially stayed there every night since the rest of E12 found out, claiming the bottom bunk under Zander for his own.

CHAPTER SIXTEEN
Alton

"I don't think this will work, for long." Alton kissed his lover.

"You're right, one of us will fall out." Paul pulled himself closer to Alton, squashed side by side onto the single bed. A hand holding on to Alton's naked hip.

"I didn't mean this." Alton rubbed his nose against Paul's affectionately and then sucked on his bottom lip.

"You said 'this'. I definitely heard you say this." Confusion showed on Paul's face.

Their naked bodies squashed together indicated this conversation would be over soon.

"I meant us sharing a room with the rest of the guys." Alton gazed into Paul's eyes. He liked what he saw there and his dick throbbed in agreement.

"Why do you say that? Don't you like them?" Paul pulled away slightly.

"No. It's not that, I love them. I think they might start to get a bit bored with us, always like this."

"This, again." Paul smiled, he swung himself up and on top, legs astride Alton. He fumbled for Alton's hands, took hold of the both and pinned them beside his head as he moved in to claim a kiss.

Alton's dick throbbed with an aching need, squashed between them. He thrust up toward Paul and felt Paul grinding against him.

All too soon Paul sat up and released his grip on Alton's hands. The cold air chilled Alton's suddenly exposed skin.

"Come back and keep me warm."

"Not until I tell you a few things." Paul's hands moved to Alton's chest, the palms covered him like two small hot blankets. "They'll let us know if we set out of line but so far we've slept in separate beds and only stolen a few private minutes alone in this room. We're a long way from overstepping the line of decency."

"So far that's true," Alton agreed. "However, this has only become my official room for two days so it's not been a long time and I'm struggling to keep my hands off you." Alton ran his hands over the ripped abs of the man in front of him.

"Oh, I see. That's a different issue." Paul's hands moved south, brushing over Alton's hips and stomach and so sensitive and twitching dick.

Alton gasped. "You said there were a few things you had to tell me."

Paul wrapped his hand around both their cocks. "I do and I don't want you to come yet, but that wasn't one of the things."

Alton's heart pounded in his chest. He watched Paul who appeared just as breathless.

"Later today you and I are going to sort out our sex life. We're going to talk to Walsh and see how we go about getting a room for just the two of us because I want to sleep in the same bed as you and fuck you in private every day. Never mind whatever we have to do for paying clients."

Alton had wondered if such a thing was possible. Alton could barely focus on the words as Paul continued to rub their dicks together. Too slowly and too gently for either of them to come but so nice.

"And this is the most important thing I want to tell you." Paul stopped. He took his hand away and lay back down atop Alton, smothering his body and covering his mouth with another kiss.

"I love you, Alton. I've loved you for such a long time but never seem to find the moment to tell you. This love makes me think about you all the time. It means you're the only person I want to be with, in this way. It means I'd do anything for you, leave here, go anywhere. And I worry about you. It also means I want everyone to know about us. You are mine and I belong to you and together we are a team."

Just for a moment, Alton forgot about sex, so amazed was he by the speech. He grinned, even though tears fell from his eyes.

"Sometimes this love thing feels overwhelming. Are you okay with it?" Paul asked.

Before Alton could answer there was a knock at the door. He turned to face the wall as the tears wouldn't stop flowing.

Paul pulled up the covers to hide them and called out, "Who is it?"

"Sorry lads, I need to get something." It was Rayfe's voice.

"Come in, Rayfe. We're almost decent."

The door opened and Alton heard his roommate more clearly.

"I'm sorry. I should have taken it before. I don't want to interrupt you too. You know the rest of us really want you two guys to feel welcome here and to get enough alone time. We'll tease you about it, of course. But we want things to work out here. We don't want to force you out or make you guys uncomfortable."

"It's fine. And thanks."

After the sound of footfall across the wooden floor, the door shut and Alton sensed they were alone again. He turned his head to face Paul. Looking at him through tear-filled eyes.

"Before you ask, these are tears of joy. I love you too. Everything you said is just the same for me." Alton wrapped his arms around Paul and placed his hands on the man's ass.

Paul kissed him tenderly. "Do you want to go and get breakfast?"

"Oh no. I want to get fucked."

The men grinned at each other.

"I love your dirty mind but there are no locks on these doors," Paul stated. "Rayfe knocked but anyone could walk in. Especially someone who doesn't know about us."

"They'd get a shock. Unfortunately, let's meet Walsh later like you suggested, and now a hand job will do."

"Only the very best for the man I love." Paul reached down between them and took hold of both of their dicks together. "I fucking need you too."

Alton had said what he had to say, what he needed to tell Paul, and heard what he needed to hear. He'd made it to West Beach.

He saw Paul's destiny, in the expression on his face.

Love, desire, ecstasy and sheer happiness and the delightful physical sensation of a hand on his cock. Paul's hand on their cocks. They were going to come together again. Feelings and emotions bled into each other until they were indistinguishable and overwhelming.

Alton was overwhelmed, loved, fucked.

The Last Three Men
by Helen J Perry

About This Story:

In a matriarchal future, far, far away a wealthy businesswoman pays for what she wants, and what she wants is confident young men to entertain her.

She selects three young men. The first two were irresistible, cool, and confident, both were tall, dark, and smoldering. In other words, exactly her type. The third man was not her type at all, but he was a part of their three-man team.

There are some things money can't buy. Men and women are segregated. A real relationship is out of the question; there can be nothing beyond fleeting encounters.

The Last Three Men

When I raised the cup to my mouth, I smelled the sugary sweetness before tasting a drop. With closed eyes, I inhaled deeply, in no hurry to devour the liquid treat.

Holding the drink inches from me, I said, "I don't know how you do it, but this is better than sex."

Ms. Setchel chuckled. "Perhaps I missed my true calling in life."

Laughing, along with the governor of the institution. I placed the cup down on the table to delay the gratification. "Oh absolutely. You should've opened a Hot Chocolate Drinking

Parlor for the elite ladies who can afford to pay for such decadent drinks. You would've made a fortune."

Cocoa and sugar had become rare precious ingredients since the virus, I didn't know how she procured them. She didn't have a cup of the delicious drink herself, I suspected it might have been only offered to the very best customers: women like me.

She smiled, but her eyes betrayed the fact that we weren't friends. She was a ruthless woman who, here in this unit, protected something even more special than chocolate.

The unit housed the rare potential to continue our species since the virus had destroyed most of the population.

She had what I wanted.

MEN.

There were so few men alive that they were enclosed and protected to ensure the future of humankind.

As a single, hard-working business woman I've earned my right to indulge in a little of what I fancy. Even if what I desire is a little taboo these days.

There has been a program to control and repress women's natural urges through a combination of brainwashing techniques and drugs. Brainwashing doesn't work, not really. Women still have lustful thoughts but don't admit to them. They are embarrassed and ashamed of them.

The successful suppression of the libido is down to the chemicals added to the water supply.

Living miles out of town, I have stuck to my well water. I'm not ready to give up on erotic fantasy and passion just yet. And I have the resources to secure what I want.

What I want is a man when I want him. And better still, one who isn't around to annoy me when I don't.

I can afford to indulge my desires in every way possible.

The arrangement is mutually beneficial to myself and the governor of the men's unit. She treats me to a hot cup of drinking chocolate to cement our deal.

The men benefit too.

They are too valuable and too rare to risk any kind of harm falling upon them. They are contained within this former prison building, for their own safety. They are kept separate from women. They aren't exposed to the potentially poisonous water that is laced with libido suppressing chemicals. Their libidos aren't suppressed and they have unmet needs and desires.

Ms. Setchel shows no reaction when I tell her I want to choose a few men from a group. Most women don't get to see men at all these days, so it may seem greedy. It should be fun for all involved.

"I'd like at least twelve men under the age of thirty, initially, from which I'll select a small group."

There was no reaction at all from Ms. Setchel.

In the modern world, anything was possible for a woman with enough wealth to pay for it. Within certain boundaries. Unfortunately, whatever happened it had to happen here within the secure walls of the unit.

"I want them to audition. It will give me a chance to get to know them a little and assess their personalities before we all go into one of those rooms for sexy times."

Ms. Setchel set it up.

The men were invited to audition. They were given no guidance on how to impress me. I wanted to see what they thought a woman in her thirties would want.

I watched from behind one-way glass, so they wouldn't see me.

The first man, Mike, was perfect.

I could have stopped there but the auditions of twelve men were all part of my evening's entertainment, I was in no hurry to get my hands on the winners. I am patient.

You would be surprised at how many men will get out their dicks when hoping to impress a woman and hoping things will quickly progress to sex. I like dicks, of course, but there is a time and place, and this wasn't it.

In the audition, other men talked. They made promises about what they would do with me given the opportunity, it was interesting to hear what a young man thinks a woman's fantasies are.

Dancing and acrobatic skills were also displayed. The audition attracted show offs.

It turned out Mike was among the oldest in the group, he was just a couple of years younger than me.

Mike strutted into the room with all the confidence of a mature man, the sort I usually go for. Did he try to impress me? No, he just stood there, sure of himself not trying to show me anything, or tell me anything, or promise he could do tricks; nothing like that. He was just there, and if I wanted to find out more about this cocky guy, I'd have to chase him. I liked that. He looked good and kept some mystery about him.

What clinched the deal, what really got my interest was when he said he was here with the dream team. I made a note of his name but decided to judge him on the performance of the team as a whole.

After Mike, I saw lots of other men, and I'm sure any one of them would have been nice enough. A group of them would've been even better. But it was difficult for any of them to impress me when they followed Mike. That was until Ezra.

Without him saying a word, I knew instantly Ezra was part of the dream team by the way he swaggered confidently into the room.

Staring into the one way glass as if he could see through it, he looked at me as if *I* were lucky to be there. He postured a little and then told me his name. By their similar appearance, Ezra and Mike were like brothers. They were both tall and slim, with dark Mediterranean looks and a presentation that oozed sex appeal.

Their presentation was professional and appeared rehearsed.

I had to wait for the penultimate audition before seeing the third man. All the while I waited, I wondered if the third man in their team would be the same.

He was not.

When Luke walked in he was all blond hair and smiles.

He had the face of an angel, youthful and innocent. Even though he was gorgeous, I couldn't picture him as a dirty playmate. Luke wouldn't have been an instant choice for me. I watched him stand in the middle of the room and, like the rest of the team, he didn't attempt to impress me with chat, or acrobatic skills, or the size of his dick.

All the dream team displayed their confidence, which suggested to me they might be red hot in the bedroom. They had *ME* begging for more!

And as they must have coordinated this audition with no notice at all this suggested they might work well together in the private room.

Luke stood in silence, with a big grin on his face.

After a while, it dawned on me, a minute is a long time to stand in front of a stranger, to just stand and say nothing. All credit where it's due, this team showed guts and creativity.

With balls like that, what else could I look forward to?

How could I not choose them?

I conveyed my choice to the officer in charge. Ms. Setchel didn't get involved in the nitty-gritty.

I waited in my room for the dream team to come knocking, and they arrived far sooner than I expected.

I welcomed them in and offered them a drink.

The three men all stood politely, and I didn't invite them to sit, I was curious to see how things would play out if I didn't dish out instructions. I gave orders all day in the outside world and welcomed the opportunity to relinquish control for a while.

"You three were all so mysterious I had to find out more, such as, which of you is the best at kissing?"

"I'm sure we all are, but we don't have to take it in turns." The young blond winked. He was eager. The other two were cooler.

"Two things I want to ask you," I said. "Firstly, are you the youngest of this team?"

Blondie gulped, he was not expecting that. Funny how you can be ready to have sex with someone but innocuous questions can catch you off guard.

"No. I'm twenty-three," he replied and pointed to another man. "He's the youngest."

My focus switched to the younger man. He was gorgeous. His blue eyes contrasted with his dark hair.

I looked back at Blondie; I do remember his name, Luke, "Secondly, what do you mean about not taking it in turns kissing?"

"We'd love to kiss you all over, and we can do that together."

I'm sure if a pussy could gulp with excitement mine just did.

"Oh, I like the sound of that. Let's get started." I leaned forward and kissed him. Drawing close to his warm body, I sensed the strength of his toned physique under his shirt. I drank in the pleasant manly flavor of his aroma.

A second mouth nibbled at the back of my neck. Unfortunately, it was almost tickling, and also it conjured vampires to my mind so it was not as erotic as it should have been, but that was not his fault.

The third man picked up my hand and kissed the back of it very tenderly, this was sweet. It gave me high hopes for the rest of the night.

I was not disappointed.

This first phase of petting all happened right by the door.

The neck-nuzzling soon stopped.

I pulled away from Blondie, at the same time the man attached to my hand said, "Let's go over to the bedroom."

It was all one big bedroom called a suite because there was a sitting area and a separate part with a bed in it.

There was no need to reply. I let the boys lead me to the bed. They asked me to lie down, so I did, and they assumed various positions around me. This is when it started getting really interesting.

I lay back, and Ezra sealed his lips against mine. My, what an expert kisser. Passion burned in his eyes, and I tasted it, like fire in his mouth. There was someone very wild and exciting inside there and yet he was restrained.

I couldn't just focus on Ezra, however, as there was a mouth making love to my fingers, that is the only way to describe it. A tongue, as well as lips, explored every inch of my hands, sucking my fingers into a mouth. Sucking and licking as if he were at my lady parts, and a teasing reminder of what was to come.

The third man kissed my feet in the same way. I wore footless tights underneath my long black dress, and my feet were bare when I invited the boys into the suite.

So far, they only touched the parts of my body that were already exposed but made an outstanding job of it. If they were to touch me like this all over, I was in for a treat better than drinking hot chocolate.

"Let's get some clothes off," one of them said. I can't say which one because the three handsome young men worked in unison, and it was all a blur.

To my delight, they kept their clothes on, while they pulled off my tights and panties. My dress stayed in place but rolled up to my stomach. They seemed so powerful and in control while I was exposed and surrounded by youths, all of them looking down at my body.

Within minutes, I had gone from being a woman in charge of an empire to feeling vulnerable and indecent. Something I rarely experience outside of the bedroom.

The decadence thrilled me.

My temperature rose whether from mild embarrassment or arousal was unclear.

One of them, Luke, pushed his way between my legs forcing them apart and exposing my cunny. His fingers hovered above it, almost touching, and the anticipation was breathtaking. Should boys his age be able to do things like this, and do them so well?

The two dark men joined me on the bed, lying either side of me. Their hands explored my body over the top of my dress and burrowed underneath it. They took it in turns to kiss my face, my neck, my mouth, and ears.

I lost my concentration.

Just as I had forgotten about Blondie and what he was about to do, he did it. His wet tongue connected with my hard clit and it felt electrifying. My pelvis moved towards his face of its own accord, at that time his fingers entered inside me. He knew what I wanted. There wasn't just one finger, and it wasn't gentle. He judged it just right and thrust hard, perhaps three or four fingers in.

Oh god, I wanted cock. I hoped these boys were well hung.

Being ravished by three handsome men, all fully dressed, and in control, while I was not, turned me on even more. Picturing what was happening in that room was as erotic as being a part of the scene.

"You want to be fucked, don't you," a voice growled in my ear.

"Fucked by three men, one after the other," said another husky voice.

"Taking it in turns."

Oh my, that is exactly what I wanted.

They took the dirty thoughts out of my head and said them out loud to me.

They worked as a team.

They had me.

I wanted more and more from them, which is how it should be.

Do not give me too much too soon.

"You enjoy turning us on don't you."

Yes, I do. I liked the fact that three young guys can be so turned on with me between them. It made me feel sexy.

"My cock is aching to get inside you."

With my eyes tightly shut, I listened to their voices and felt all that they were doing to me and more. I sensed what they were offering. The voices, the words, the touches, they were almost too much.

"Are you going to fuck her Luke? Or do you want to make way for me?"

Now, I was ten years older than the youngest of them and I was the wealthy owner of a big business. It was exciting to hear these men talk like that about me. At last, some people who don't stop and deferentially ask me what they should be doing next.

From the slight sounds and the way the bed was bouncing, I sensed Luke moving about and guessed he was getting his cock out, and judging by the sound of a crinkling wrapped, sorting a condom.

I couldn't see what Luke was doing because Mike was in my mouth again, he had me pinned down with a passionate kiss.

The fabric of Luke's clothes brushed against my inner thighs, and he hadn't removed his pants completely, just shoved them down.

I tried to imagine his erect cock. How big was it? I soon found out. Something much bigger than his fingers, pushed to enter me and met little resistance.

I wanted to groan, but a face, teeth, and tongue blocked my mouth.

A big cock was thrusting in and out, the movements were slow but long. He pulled completely out and pushed back in all the way, it was a long way. Oh my, his cock was at least as big as I imagined.

Where was the third man? No longer beside me. My quim received more attention than just one lover could deliver.

Hands were on my stomach, on my buttocks, on my breasts.

Fingers intruded between my body and the man fucking me and touched my throbbing clit. Those fingers danced around my sensitive labia. More fingers working their way around my hole.

Was Ezra touching my pussy and Luke's dick as he fucked me? *How erotic!* The wandering hands moved from my dripping pussy, rubbed along the slit, towards my perineum, my arse. I felt fingers slippery with my juices, penetrating my rear.

Are the three men going to fuck me there too? What a team.

That was it. That was more sensations than my body could take. I mustered all my strength to push this man off my mouth, I needed to breathe when I came, and I needed to come right then.

Unstoppable heat and pleasures of the senses overwhelmed me. The guys stepped up the perfect pressure and rhythm to please me and carry me through my orgasm.

As the waves of the climax subsided a little, I looked into Luke's blue eyes. The boyish grin had gone, and I saw an experienced sexual athlete who was as aroused as I was and he was about to come too. This, and his frantic thrusting was enough to bring me to the height of another orgasm and we came together.

There was no collapsing into each other's arms, which would have spoilt the moment.

Our menage was just sex, we couldn't afford cuddles, and emotional attachment and they all knew it.

Damn it. They were as deprived as me. Just as I lacked male company in my daily life, they were prisoners in a world without women.

I shook such thoughts from my head. I had to stay in the moment.

Climax completed, Luke climbed off me ready to turn his hand to something else and let another man take his place.

As he moved away, I saw Ezra behind him, flies already open and a huge hard cock already out. He was rolling on a condom. He looked up at me and smiled, the smile of a man with a dirty and adventurous mind. I recognized a kindred spirit.

"How are you are going to fuck me?" I asked, "You're not just going to just follow your friend are you?" I taunted him to make sure we were on the same grubby page.

"I'm going to give you what you want," he replied, with bags of that sure-of-himself confidence that hooked me on to him and Mike straight away.

He lifted my legs in the air. Ezra helped to raise my legs into the right position, legs up almost in a fetal position, yet on my back. My pussy and arse were completely exposed. I watched him, and he stared right back at me as he probed the edge of my drenched pussy with his rubber-encased cock and then pushed it down the crack between my cheeks to push gently on that hole.

I noticed a tube of lube in his hands. He made a big display of emptying it on to his fingers. These actions made it clear to both of us what he planned for my backside. And when I say planned I mean planned. I hadn't seen him move to get the lube, it must have been handy all the while, perhaps in his pocket.

Totally focused on Ezra, the others were almost forgotten, when I glanced at them, they were both standing by and watching.

Mike rubbed a huge bulge in the front of his jeans.

Luke had tucked himself away, he looked very sexy and didn't appear to have lost interest. His eyes were wide watching the action between my legs.

I suspected he liked seeing Ezra's cock, well, not for much longer. *Bury that cock in me*, I willed him.

My attention was brought back to Ezra, and I automatically shut my eyes and fingers slid into my rear hole.

It felt so good, and Ezra knew it. He kept his fingers in there, but I was aware of him readying his cock at the entrance with his free hand. When he pulled out his fingers, his cock slid in slowly, inch by lovely inch.

Ezra held still once inside, giving my body the chance to adjust and accept this new sensation of being totally filled.

"Relax," he whispered, the words seemed gentle in contrast to the almost brutal way my body was being used.

Used wasn't the right word, pleasured would be more accurate. "Take deep breaths, slow and steady with me."

Oh wow, as we harmonized our breathing our entire bodies began to work together. Ezra started to thrust in time with our panting and this, the youngest man, was performing as well as any of the men.

"Are you guys just watching now?" he asked, his question directed at his team, ignoring me.

Unprofessional perhaps?

No. It was perfect.

In that moment he broke the intimate bond between us and reminded me we were engaged in debauchery and putting on an exhibition. And he invited them to join in.

Everything about these three men and the way they made me theirs was sexy.

The two spare men both jumped into action.

Luke held one of my legs, helping to change my position slightly. Mike went to the other side and held the other leg. This made things far more comfortable for me, but he didn't stop there. "Ezra, if you aren't going to fuck her cunt then do you mind if I do?"

"Go ahead," replied Ezra.

More of the team banter: I liked it.

My mind was going to explode if only these two hunks would fuck me at the same time.

Fingers entered my pussy, fingers were on my clit, and a cock was fucking my behind.

Too much. Sensation overload. I thrust so hard I was going to remember this for days but it felt so good. The orgasm was like nothing I could remember from before.

The men were relentless, even when I came and came again.

They fucked me until I begged them to stop.

Although they were friendly, all three of them kept an aloof professional manner throughout, they never undressed.

They were professional and enigmatic to the very end.

Too professional. Too mysterious. I wanted them to like me and I couldn't figure it out.

But they weren't prostitutes.

I had paid for their company, sure. I had to bribe my way into this unit. Beyond that, I wanted them, they also wanted me. They'd freely chosen to audition. They wanted to do this. They'd even chosen their comrades, the team: the dream team.

They gave me everything I wanted, physically, but I wanted to know the men better. I'd give anything to make that a possibility. I'd have to change the world.

The men were well treated and protected within the unit, but it resembled a prison. For their own safety, they weren't allowed to leave.

Any chance of a real rounded relationship with a man right now was only fantasy. Living with a man was an impossible dream.

Perhaps they'd kept an emotional distance to protect themselves. Perhaps they wanted more, but feared it wasn't possible.

"I think you wanted to be fucked by three cocks at once, we can do that to you, just ask us next time," Ezra said to me.

How does a twenty-year-old come up with stuff like that?

"I had to bribe my way in here. What if I can't do it again?"

The three men exchanged glances and some form of silent communication took place before they all nodded to each other. They crowded around me.

Mike whispered in my ear. "What would you say if I told you we had an escape plan? We'd like to meet you on the outside." He was so quiet I barely heard him.

I giggled. It had to be a ruse. But they all seemed so serious.

"We have a way out, but nowhere to go and no one to help us on the outside," Luke whispered.

The other men glared at him. I guess he'd said too much.

"What makes you think you can trust me to help and not report you?"

Ezra regained his composure quickly. "Two things. You seem to be on the same wavelength as us.."

The comment warmed me.

"And, secondly, you can't report anything just yet because you don't know our plan."

Mike's arm went around my shoulder as he wrapped me in a friendly embrace. "We all have a really good feeling about you, Rosie. I'd be surprised if we are wrong. We four go together so well. Didn't you think so?"

I nodded. I had to admit we did.

"We don't want to live here for the rest of our lives. And you don't want to be restricted to visiting us when you can bribe your way in, either. There's more to life, Rosie."

I wanted to believe them. They were painting the fantasy for me as if they'd seen inside my mind.

"Are you just saying this to me because you need a woman on the outside?"

"Hell, no. Far from it." Luke sounded indignant. "We could've asked any woman. We do meet quite a few here, one way or another. But we're quite self-sufficient. We were planning to get far from the towns and make our own way."

"But," Mike interrupted. "Meeting you here like this has to be luck or fate or something. You seem different to every woman we're met. We're all wondering if things can work out better for all of us together."

"What do I have to do to help you escape?"

"Nothing. Just give us your address and we'll come and find you in a few days."

Also by H J Perry

Eurydice Chronicles
Warrior

Gay Footballer Romance
My Goal
Home Goal

Gay Sci Fi Romance Soulmates
Promised to Idris
Fighting With Aaron
Soul [Gay Sci Fi Soulmates]
Marked by Kane

Sky High Scaffolders
Our Secret Wedding
Our Secret Christmas

Tread the Boards
A Secret Boyfriend
Friends With Benefits
The Glass Ceiling: A Second Chance Romance

Standalone

Rescued From Paradise
Arrival: Gay Romance in a Post Apocalyptic Dystopian Society
Streets Apart & Hearts Apart
Christmas in Wonderland
The Prince and The Bodyguard

Watch for more at https://helenjperry.com/.

About the Author

HJ Perry lives in the English countryside BUT is learning to accept having words translated into American for an international audience. Having worked in the construction industry for years in real life, her fictional characters also often work in that macho, male-dominated environment.

HJP has also been a political activist campaigning around LBGT issues since the 1980s.

She enjoys visiting museums, watching films, and live theatre. But most of her spare time she spends reading. You will find lust, sex, desire, and love in her books. They are for an adult audience.

Read more at https://helenjperry.com/.